William James Rolfe, Robert Carruthers, Thomas Gray

Select Poems of Thomas Gray

Vol. 1

William James Rolfe, Robert Carruthers, Thomas Gray

Select Poems of Thomas Gray
Vol. 1

ISBN/EAN: 9783337407438

Printed in Europe, USA, Canada, Australia, Japan

Cover: Foto ©Andreas Hilbeck / pixelio.de

More available books at **www.hansebooks.com**

your humble Serv[t] F: Gray

SELECT POEMS

OF

THOMAS GRAY.

EDITED, WITH NOTES,

BY

WILLIAM J. ROLFE, A.M.,

FORMERLY HEAD MASTER OF THE HIGH SCHOOL, CAMBRIDGE, MASS.

PREFACE.

MANY editions of Gray have been published in the last fifty years, some of them very elegant, and some showing considerable editorial labor, but not one, so far as I am aware, critically exact either in text or in notes. No editor since Mathias (A.D. 1814) has given the 2d line of the *Elegy* as Gray wrote and printed it ; while Mathias's mispunctuation of the 123d line has been copied by his successors, almost without exception. Other variations from the early editions are mentioned in the notes.

It is a curious fact that the most accurate edition of Gray's collected poems is the *editio princeps* of 1768, printed under his own supervision. The first edition of the two Pindaric odes, *The Progress of Poesy* and *The Bard* (Strawberry-Hill, 1757), was printed with equal care, and the proofs were probably read by the poet. The text of the present edition has been collated, line by line, with that of these early editions, and in but one instance (*Elegy*, 35) have I adopted a later reading. All the MS. variations, and the various readings I have noted in the modern editions, are given in the notes.

Pickering's edition of 1835, edited by Mitford, has been followed blindly in nearly all the more recent editions, and its many errors (see pp. 84 and 105, foot-notes) have been faithfully reproduced. Even its blunders in the "indenting" of the lines in the corresponding stanzas of the two Pindaric odes, which any careful proof-reader ought to have corrected, have been copied again and again—as in the Boston (1853) reprint of Pickering, the pretty little edition of Bickers & Son (London, n. d.), the fac-simile of the latter printed at our University Press, Cambridge (1866), etc.

Of former editions of Gray, the only one very fully annotated is Mitford's (Pickering, 1835), already mentioned. I have drawn freely from that, correcting many errors, and also from Wakefield's and Mason's editions, and from Hales's notes (*Longer English Poems*, London, 1872) on the *Elegy* and the Pindaric odes. To all this material many original notes and illustrations have been added.

The facts concerning the first publication of the *Elegy* are not given correctly by any of the editors, and even the "experts" of *Notes and*

Queries have not been able to disentangle the snarl of conflicting evidence.   I am not sure that I have settled the question myself (see p. 74 and foot-note), but I have at least shown that Gray is a more credible witness in the case than any of his critics.   Their testimony is obviously inconsistent and inconclusive ; he may have confounded the names of two magazines, but that remains to be proved.*

I have retained most of the "parallel passages" from the poets given by the editors, and have added others, without regard to the critics who have sneered at this kind of annotations.   Whether Gray borrowed from the others, or the others from him, matters little ; very likely, in most instances, neither party was consciously the borrower.   Gray, in his own notes, has acknowledged certain debts to other poets, and probably these were all that he was aware of.   Some of these he contracted unwittingly (see what he says of one of them in a letter to Walpole, quoted in the note on the *Ode on the Spring*, 31), and the same may have been true of some apparently similar cases pointed out by modern editors.   To me, however, the chief interest of these coincidences and resemblances of thought or expression is as studies in the "comparative anatomy" of poetry.   The teacher will find them useful as pegs to hang questions upon, or texts for oral instruction.   The pupil, or the young reader, who finds out who all these poets were, when they lived, what they wrote, etc., will have learned no small amount of English literary history.   If he studies the quotations merely as illustrations of style and expression, or as examples of the poetic diction of various periods, he will have learned some lessons in the history and the use of his mother-tongue.

The wood-cuts on pp. 9, 25, 26, 27, 28, 30, 34, 36, 39, 40, 41, 42, 43, 50, and 61 are from Birket Foster's designs ; those on pp. 29, 31, 33, 35, 37, and 38 are from the graceful drawings of "E. V. B." (the Hon. Mrs. Boyle) ; the rest are from various sources.

Cambridge, Feb. 29, 1876.

---

* Since writing the above to-day, I have found by the merest chance in my own library another bit of evidence in the case, which fully confirms my surmise that the *Elegy* was printed in *The Magazine of Magazines* before it appeared in the *Grand Magazine of Magazines.*   Chambers's *Book of Days* (vol. ii. p. 146), in an article on "Gray and his Elegy," says :

"It first saw the light in *The Magazine of Magazines*, February, 1751.   Some imaginary literary wag is made to rise in a convivial assembly, and thus announce it : ' Gentlemen, give me leave to soothe my own melancholy, and amuse you in a most noble manner, with a full copy of verses by the very ingenious Mr. Gray, of Peterhouse, Cambridge. They are stanzas written in a country churchyard.'   Then follow the verses.   A few days afterwards, Dodsley's edition appeared," etc.

The same authority gives the four stanzas omitted after the 18th (see p. 79) as they appear in the *North American Review*, except that the first line of the third is " Hark how the sacred calm that *reigns* around," a reading which I have found nowhere else. The stanza "There scattered oft," etc. (p. 81), is given as in the review.   The reading on p. 82 must be a later one.

STOKE-POGIS CHURCH.

THE LIFE OF THOMAS GRAY.

By Robert Carruthers.

THOMAS GRAY, the author of the celebrated *Elegy written in a Country Churchyard*, was born in Cornhill, London, December 26, 1716. His father, Philip Gray, an exchange broker and scrivener, was a wealthy and nominally respectable citizen, but he treated his family with brutal severity and neglect, and the poet was altogether indebted for the advantages of a learned education to the affectionate care and industry of his mother, whose maiden name was Antrobus, and who, in conjunction with a maiden sister, kept a millinery shop. A brother of Mrs. Gray was assistant to the Master of Eton, and was also a fellow of Pembroke College, Cambridge. Under his protection the poet was educated at Eton, and from thence went to Peterhouse, attending college from 1734 to September, 1738. At Eton he had as contemporaries Richard West, son of the Lord Chancellor of Ireland, and Horace Walpole, son of the triumphant Whig minister, Sir Robert Walpole. West died early in his 26th year, but his genius and virtues and his sorrows will forever live in the correspondence of his friend. In the spring of 1739, Gray was invited by Horace Walpole to accompany him as travelling companion in a tour through France and Italy. They made the usual route, and Gray wrote remarks on all he saw in Florence, Rome, Naples, etc. His observations on arts and antiquities, and his sketches of foreign manners, evince his admirable taste, learning, and discrimination. Since Milton, no such accomplished English traveller had visited those classic shores. In their journey through Dauphiny, Gray's attention was strongly arrested by the wild and picturesque site of the Grande Chartreuse, surrounded by its dense forest of beech and fir, its enormous precipices, cliffs, and cascades. He visited it a second time on his return, and in the album of the mountain convent he wrote his famous Alcaic Ode. At Reggio the travellers quarrelled and parted. Walpole took the whole blame on himself. He was fond of pleasure and amusements, "intoxicated by vanity, indulgence, and the insolence of his situation as a prime minister's son"—his own confession—while Gray was studious, of a serious disposition, and independent spirit. The immediate cause of the rupture is said to have been Walpole's clandestinely opening, reading, and resealing a letter addressed to Gray, in which he expected to find a confirmation of his suspicions that Gray had been writing unfavourably of him to some friends in England. A partial reconciliation was effected about three years afterwards by the intervention of a lady, and Walpole redeemed his youthful error by a life-long sincere admiration and respect for his friend. From Reggio Gray proceeded to Venice, and thence travelled homewards, attended by a *laquais de voyage.* He arrived in England in September, 1741, having been absent about two years and a half. His father died in November, and it was found that the poet's fortune would not enable him to prosecute the study of the law. He therefore retired to Cambridge, and fixed his residence at the university. There he continued for the remainder of his life, with the exception of about two years spent in London, when the treasures of the British Museum were thrown open. At Cambridge he had the range of noble libraries. His happiness consisted in study, and he perused with critical attention the Greek and Roman poets, philosophers, historians, and orators. Plato and the Anthologia he read and annotated with great care, as if for publication. He compiled tables of Greek chronology, added notes to Linnæus and other naturalists, wrote geographical disquisitions on Strabo ; and, besides being familiar with French and Italian literature, was a zealous archæological student, and profoundly versed in architecture, botany, painting, and music. In all departments of human learning, except mathematics, he was a master. But it follows that one so studious, so critical, and so fastidious, could not be a voluminous writer. A few poems include all the original compositions of Gray—the quintessence, as it were, of thirty years of ceaseless study and contemplation, irradiated by bright and fitful gleams of inspiration. In 1742 Gray composed his *Ode to Spring*, his *Ode on a Distant Prospect of Eton College*, and his *Ode to Adversity*—productions which most readers of poetry can repeat from memory. He commenced a didactic poem, *On the Alliance of Education and Government*, but wrote only about a hundred lines. Every reader must regret that this philosophical poem is but a fragment. It is in the style and measure of Dryden, of whom Gray was an ardent admirer and close student. His *Elegy written in a Country Churchyard* was completed and published in 1751. In the form of a sixpenny *brochure* it circulated rapidly, four editions being exhausted the first year. This popularity surprised the poet. He said sarcastically that it was owing entirely to the subject, and that the public would have received it as well if it had been written in prose. The solemn and affecting nature of the poem, applicable to all ranks and classes, no doubt aided its sale ; it required high poetic sensibility and a cultivated taste to appreciate the rapid transitions, the figurative language, and lyrical magnificence of the odes ; but the elegy went home to all hearts ; while its musical harmony, originality, and pathetic train of sentiment and feeling render it one of the most perfect of English poems. No vicissitudes of taste or fashion have affected its popularity. When the original manuscript of the poem was lately (1854) offered for sale, it brought the almost incredible sum of £131. The two great odes of Gray, *The Progress of Poetry* and *The Bard*, were published in 1757, and were but coldly received. His name, however, stood high, and on the death of Cibber, the same year, he was offered the laureateship, which he wisely declined. He was ambitious, however, of obtaining the more congenial and dignified appointment of Professor of Modern History in the University of Cambridge, which fell vacant in 1762, and, by the advice of his friends, he made application to Lord Bute, but was unsuccessful. Lord Bute had designed it for the tutor of his son-in-law, Sir James Lowther. No one had heard of the tutor, but the Bute influence was all-prevailing. In 1765 Gray took a journey into Scotland, penetrating as far north as Dunkeld and the Pass of Killiecrankie ; and his account of his tour, in letters to his friends, is replete with interest and with touches of his peculiar humour and graphic description. One other poem proceeded from his pen. In 1768 the Professorship of Modern History was again vacant, and the Duke of Grafton bestowed it upon Gray. A sum of £400 per annum was thus added to his income ; but his health was precarious—he had lost it, he said, just when he began to be easy in his circumstances. The nomination of the Duke of Grafton to the office of Chancellor of the University enabled Gray to acknowledge the favour

conferred on himself. He thought it better that gratitude
should sing than expectation, and he honoured his grace's installation with an ode. Such occasional productions are seldom happy; but Gray preserved his poetic dignity and select
beauty of expression. He made the founders of Cambridge,
as Mr. Hallam has remarked, "pass before our eyes like
shadows over a magic glass." When the ceremony of the
installation was over, the poet-professor went on a tour to
the lakes of Cumberland and Westmoreland, and few of the
beauties of the lake-country, since so famous, escaped his ob-
servation. This was to be his last excursion. While at din-
ner one day in the college-hall he was seized with an attack
of gout in his stomach, which resisted all the powers of med-
icine, and proved fatal in less than a week. He died on the
30th of July, 1771, and was buried, according to his own desire, beside the remains of his mother at Stoke-Pogis, near
Slough, in Buckinghamshire, in a beautiful sequestered village
churchyard that is supposed to have furnished the scene of
his elegy.* The literary habits and personal peculiarities

* A claim has been put up for the churchyard of Granchester, about
two miles from Cambridge, the great bell of St. Mary's serving for the
"curfew." But Stoke-Pogis is more likely to have been the spot, if any
individual locality were indicated. The poet often visited the village, his
aunt and mother residing there, and his aunt was interred in the churchyard of the place. Gray's epitaph on his mother is characterized not only
by the tenderness with which he always regarded her memory, but by his
style and cast of thought. It runs thus: "Beside her friend and sister
here sleep the remains of Dorothy Gray, widow, the careful, tender mother
of many children, one of whom alone had the misfortune to survive her.
She died March 11, 1753, aged 72." She had lived to read the *Elegy*,
which was perhaps an ample recompense for her maternal cares and affection. Mrs. Gray's will commences in a similar touching strain: "In
the name of God, amen. This is the last will and desire of Dorothy Gray
to her son Thomas Gray." [Cunningham's edit. of *Johnson's Lives.*]
They were all in all to each other. The father's cruelty and neglect, their
straitened circumstances, the sacrifices made by the mother to maintain
her son at the university, her pride in the talents and conduct of that son,
and the increasing gratitude and affection of the latter, nursed in his scho-

of Gray are familiar to us from the numerous representations and allusions of his friends. It is easy to fancy the recluse-poet sitting in his college-chambers in the old quadrangle of Pembroke Hall. His windows are ornamented with mignonette and choice flowers in China vases, but outside may be discerned some iron-work intended to be serviceable as a fire-escape, for he has a horror of fire. His furniture is neat and select ; his books, rather for use than show, are disposed around him. He has a harpsichord in the room. In the corner of one of the apartments is a trunk containing his deceased mother's dresses, carefully folded up and preserved. His fastidiousness, bordering upon effeminacy, is visible in his gait and manner—in his handsome features and small, well-dressed person, especially when he walks abroad and sinks the author and hard student in "the gentleman who sometimes writes for his amusement." He writes always with a crow-quill, speaks slowly and sententiously, and shuns the crew of dissonant college revellers, who call him "a prig," and seek to annoy him. Long mornings of study, and nights feverish from ill-health, are spent in those chambers ; he is often listless and in low spirits ; yet his natural temper is not desponding, and he delights in employment. He has always something to learn or to communicate—some sally of humour or quiet stroke of satire for his

lastic and cloistered solitude—these form an affecting but noble record in the history of genius.

[One would infer from the above that Mrs. Gray was *not* "interred in the churchyard of the place," though the epitaph given immediately after shows that she *was*. Gray in his will directed that he should be laid beside her there. The passage in the will reads thus : "First, I do desire that my body may be deposited in the vault, made by my dear mother in the churchyard of Stoke-Pogeis, near Slough in Buckinghamshire, by her remains, in a coffin of seasoned oak, neither lined nor covered, and (unless it be inconvenient) I could wish that one of my executors may see me laid in the grave, and distribute among such honest and industrious poor persons in said parish as he thinks fit, the sum of ten pounds in charity."—*Ed.*]

friends and correspondents—some note on natural history to enter in his journal—some passage of Plato to unfold and illustrate—some golden thought of classic inspiration to inlay on his page—some bold image to tone down—some verse to retouch and harmonize. His life is on the whole innocent and happy, and a feeling of thankfulness to the Great Giver is breathed over all.

Various editions of the collected works of Gray have been published. The first, including memoirs of his life and his correspondence, edited by his friend, the Rev. W. Mason, appeared in 1775. It has been often reprinted, and forms the groundwork of the editions by Mathias (1814) and Mitford (1816). Mr. Mitford, in 1843, published Gray's correspondence with the Rev. Norton Nicholls; and in 1854 another collection of Gray's letters was published, edited also by Mr. Mitford. Every scrap of the poet's MSS. is eagerly sought after, and every year seems to add to his popularity as a poet and letter-writer.

———

In 1778 a monument to Gray was erected in Westminster Abbey by Mason, with the following inscription :

> No more the Grecian muse unrivall'd reigns,
> To Britain let the nations homage pay ;
> She felt a Homer's fire in Milton's strains,
> A Pindar's rapture in the lyre of Gray.

The cenotaph afterwards erected in Stoke Park by Mr. Penn is described below.

WEST-END HOUSE.

STOKE-POGIS.

FROM HOWITT'S "HOMES AND HAUNTS OF THE BRITISH POETS."*

It is at Stoke-Pogis that we seek the most attractive vestiges of Gray. Here he used to spend his vacations, not only when a youth at Eton, but during the whole of his future life, while his mother and his aunts lived. Here it was that his *Ode on a Distant Prospect of Eton College*, his celebrated *Elegy written in a Country Churchyard*, and his *Long Story* were not only written, but were mingled with the circumstances and all the tenderest feelings of his own life.

* Harper's edition, vol. i. p. 314 foll.

His mother and aunts lived at an old-fashioned house in a very retired spot at Stoke, called West-End. This house stood in a hollow, much screened by trees. A small stream ran through the garden, and it is said that Gray used to employ himself when here much in this garden, and that many of the trees still remaining are of his planting. On one side of the house extended an upland field, which was planted round so as to give a charming retired walk; and at the summit of the field was raised an artificial mound, and upon it was built a sort of arcade or summer-house, which gave full prospect of Windsor and Eton. Here Gray used to delight to sit; here he was accustomed to read and write much; and it is just the place to inspire the *Ode on Eton College*, which lay in the midst of its fine landscape, beautifully in view. The old house inhabited by Gray and his mother has just been pulled down, and replaced by an Elizabethan mansion by the present proprietor, Mr. Penn, of Stoke Park, just by.* The garden, of course, has shared in the change, and now stands gay with its fountain and its modern greenhouse, and, excepting for some fine trees, no longer reminds you of Gray. The woodland walk still remains round the adjoining field, and the summer-house on its summit, though now much cracked by time, and only held together by iron cramps. The trees are now so lofty that they completely obstruct the view, and shut out both Eton and Windsor.

* * * * * * * * *

Stoke Park is about a couple of miles from Slough. The

* This was written (or published, at least) in 1846; but Mitford, in the Life of Gray prefixed to the "Eton edition" of his Poems, published in 1847, says: "The house, which is now called *West-End,* lies in a secluded part of the parish, on the road to Fulmer. It has lately been much enlarged and adorned by its present proprietor [Mr. Penn], but the room called 'Gray's' (distinguished by a small balcony) is still preserved; and a shady walk round an adjoining meadow, with a summer-house on the rising land, are still remembered as favourite places frequented by the poet."—*Ed.*

B

country is flat, but its monotony is broken up by the noble
character and disposition of its woods.   Near the house is a
fine expanse of water, across which the eye falls on fine views,
particularly to the south, of Windsor Castle, Cooper's Hill,
and the Forest Woods.   About three hundred yards from the
north front of the house stands a column, sixty-eight feet high,
bearing on the top a colossal statue of Sir Edward Coke, by
Rosa.   The woods of the park shut out the view of West-End
House, Gray's occasional residence, but the space is open
from the mansion across the park, so as to take in the view
both of the church and of a monument erected by the late
Mr. Penn to Gray.   Alighting from the carriage at a lodge,
we enter the park just at the monument.   This is composed
of fine freestone, and consists of a large sarcophagus, supported on a square pedestal, with inscriptions on each side.
Three of them are selected from the *Ode on Eton College* and
the *Elegy.*   They are :

> Hard by yon wood, now smiling as in scorn,
>   Muttering his wayward fancies he would rove ;
> Now drooping, woeful-wan, like one forlorn,
>   Or craz'd with care, or cross'd in hopeless love.

> One morn I miss'd him on the custom'd hill,
>   Along the heath, and near his fav'rite tree ;
> Another came ; nor yet beside the rill,
>   Nor up the lawn, nor at the wood was he.

The second is from the *Ode:*

> Ye distant spires ! ye antique towers !
>   That crown the watery glade,
> Where grateful Science still adores
>   Her Henry's holy shade ;
> And ye, that from the stately brow
> Of Windsor's heights th' expanse below
>   Of grove, of lawn, of mead survey,
> Whose turf, whose shade, whose flowers among
> Wanders the hoary Thames along
>   His silver-winding way.

Ah, happy hills ! ah, pleasing shade !
   Ah, fields belov'd in vain !
Where once my careless childhood stray'd,
   A stranger yet to pain !
I feel the gales that from ye blow,
A momentary bliss bestow.

The third is again from the *Elegy:*

Beneath those rugged elms, that yew-tree's shade,
   Where heaves the turf in many a mouldering heap,
Each in his narrow cell forever laid,
   The rude forefathers of the hamlet sleep.

The breezy call of incense-breathing morn,
   The swallow twittering from the straw-built shed,
The cock's shrill clarion or the echoing horn,
   No more shall rouse them from their lowly bed.

The fourth bears this inscription :

This Monument, in honour of
THOMAS GRAY,
Was erected A.D. 1799,
Among the scenery
Celebrated by that great Lyric and Elegiac Poet.
He died in 1771,
And lies unnoted in the adjoining Church-yard,
Under the Tomb-stone on which he piously
And pathetically recorded the interment
Of his Aunt and lamented Mother.

This monument is in a neatly kept garden-like enclosure, with a winding walk approaching from the shade of the neighbouring trees. To the right, across the park, at some little distance, backed by fine trees, stands the rural little church and churchyard where Gray wrote his *Elegy*, and where he lies. As you walk on to this, the mansion closes the distant view between the woods with fine effect. The church has often been engraved, and is therefore tolerably familiar to the general reader. It consists of two barn-like structures, with tall roofs, set side by side, and the tower and

finely tapered spire rising above them at the northwest corner.   The church is thickly hung with ivy, where

> "The moping owl may to the moon complain
> Of such as, wandering near her secret bower,
>   Molest her ancient, solitary reign."

The structure is as simple and old-fashioned, both without
and within, as any village church can well be.   No village,
however, is to be seen.   Stoke consists chiefly of scattered
houses, and this is now in the midst of the park.   In the
churchyard,

> "Beneath those rugged elms, that yew-tree's shade,
>   Where heaves the turf in many a mouldering heap,
> Each in his narrow cell forever laid,
>   The rude forefathers of the hamlet sleep."

All this is quite literal; and the tomb of the poet himself,
near the southeast window, completes the impression of the
scene.   It is a plain brick altar tomb, covered with a blue
slate slab, and, besides his own ashes, contains those of his
mother and aunt.   On the slab are inscribed the following
lines by Gray himself: "In the vault beneath are deposited,
in hope of a joyful resurrection, the remains of *Mary Antrobus.*
She died unmarried, Nov. 5, 1749, aged sixty-six.   In the same
pious confidence, beside her friend and sister, here sleep the
remains of *Dorothy Gray,* widow; the careful, tender mother
of many children, ONE of whom alone had the misfortune to
survive her.   She died, March 11, 1753, aged LXXII."

No testimony of the interment of Gray in the same tomb
was inscribed anywhere till Mr. Penn, in 1799, erected the
monument already mentioned, and placed a small slab in the
wall, under the window, opposite to the tomb itself, recording
the fact of Gray's burial there.   The whole scene is well worthy
of a summer day's stroll, especially for such as, pent in the
metropolis, know how to enjoy the quiet freshness of the country and the associations of poetry and the past.

GRAY'S MONUMENT, STOKE PARK.

ELEGY WRITTEN IN A COUNTRY CHURCHYARD.

ELEGY WRITTEN IN A COUNTRY CHURCHYARD.

THE curfew tolls the knell of parting day,
  The lowing herd wind slowly o'er the lea,
The plowman homeward plods his weary way,
  And leaves the world to darkness and to me.

Now fades the glimmering landscape on the sight,   5
  And all the air a solemn stillness holds,
Save where the beetle wheels his droning flight,
  And drowsy tinklings lull the distant folds :

Save that, from yonder ivy-mantled tower,
  The moping owl does to the moon complain   10
Of such as, wandering near her secret bower,
  Molest her ancient solitary reign.

Beneath those rugged elms, that yew-tree's shade,
   Where heaves the turf in many a mouldering heap,
Each in his narrow cell forever laid,   15
   The rude forefathers of the hamlet sleep.

The breezy call of incense-breathing morn,
   The swallow twittering from the straw-built shed,
The cock's shrill clarion, or the echoing horn,
   No more shall rouse them from their lowly bed.   20

For them no more the blazing hearth shall burn,
 Or busy housewife ply her evening care ;
No children run to lisp their sire's return,
 Or climb his knees the envied kiss to share.

Oft did the harvest to their sickle yield,   25
    Their furrow oft the stubborn glebe has broke;
How jocund did they drive their team afield!
    How bow'd the woods beneath their sturdy stroke!

Let not Ambition mock their useful toil,
   Their homely joys, and destiny obscure ;
Nor Grandeur hear with a disdainful smile
   The short and simple annals of the poor.

30

The boast of heraldry, the pomp of power,
   And all that beauty, all that wealth e'er gave,
Await alike th' inevitable hour.   35
   The paths of glory lead but to the grave.

Nor you, ye proud, impute to these the fault,
   If Memory o'er their tomb no trophies raise;
Where, through the long-drawn aisle and fretted vault,
   The pealing anthem swells the note of praise.   40

Can storied urn or animated bust
   Back to its mansion call the fleeting breath?
Can Honour's voice provoke the silent dust?
   Or Flattery soothe the dull cold ear of Death?

Perhaps in this neglected spot is laid   45
   Some heart once pregnant with celestial fire;
Hands, that the rod of empire might have sway'd,
   Or wak'd to ecstasy the living lyre:

But Knowledge to their eyes her ample page,
   Rich with the spoils of time, did ne'er unroll;   50
Chill Penury repress'd their noble rage,
   And froze the genial current of the soul.

Full many a gem of purest ray serene
   The dark unfathom'd caves of ocean bear;
Full many a flower is born to blush unseen,   55
   And waste its sweetness on the desert air.

C

Some village Hampden, that with dauntless breast
　　The little tyrant of his fields withstood,
Some mute inglorious Milton here may rest,
　　Some Cromwell, guiltless of his country's blood.　　60

Th' applause of listening senates to command,
　　The threats of pain and ruin to despise,
To scatter plenty o'er a smiling land,
　　And read their history in a nation's eyes,

Their lot forbade: nor circumscrib'd alone　　65
　　Their growing virtues, but their crimes confin'd;
Forbade to wade through slaughter to a throne,
　　And shut the gates of mercy on mankind,

The struggling pangs of conscious truth to hide,
  To quench the blushes of ingenuous shame, 70
Or heap the shrine of Luxury and Pride
  With incense kindled at the Muse's flame.

Far from the madding crowd's ignoble strife,
  Their sober wishes never learn'd to stray;
Along the cool sequester'd vale of life 75
  They kept the noiseless tenor of their way.

Yet even these bones from insult to protect,
    Some frail memorial still erected nigh,
With uncouth rhymes and shapeless sculpture deck'd,
    Implores the passing tribute of a sigh.   80

Their name, their years, spelt by th' unletter'd Muse,
    The place of fame and elegy supply;
And many a holy text around she strews,
    That teach the rustic moralist to die.

For who, to dumb forgetfulness a prey,   85
    This pleasing anxious being e'er resign'd,
Left the warm precincts of the cheerful day,
    Nor cast one longing lingering look behind?

On some fond breast the parting soul relies,
  Some pious drops the closing eye requires ;   90
Even from the tomb the voice of Nature cries,
  Even in our ashes live their wonted fires.

For thee, who, mindful of th' unhonour'd dead,
  Dost in these lines their artless tale relate,
If chance, by lonely contemplation led,   95
  Some kindred spirit shall inquire thy fate,

Haply some hoary-headed swain may say,
　"Oft have we seen him at the peep of dawn
Brushing with hasty steps the dews away,
　To meet the sun upon the upland lawn. 100

"There at the foot of yonder nodding beech,
   That wreathes its old fantastic roots so high,
His listless length at noontide would he stretch,
   And pore upon the brook that babbles by.

"Hard by yon wood, now smiling as in scorn,   105
    Muttering his wayward fancies he would rove;
Now drooping, woeful-wan, like one forlorn,
    Or craz'd with care, or cross'd in hopeless love.

"One morn I miss'd him on the custom'd hill,
    Along the heath, and near his favourite tree;   110
Another came; nor yet beside the rill,
    Nor up the lawn, nor at the wood was he;

"The next, with dirges due in sad array,
    Slow through the church-way path we saw him borne.
Approach and read (for thou canst read) the lay   115
    Grav'd on the stone beneath yon aged thorn."

THE EPITAPH.

Here rests his head upon the lap of Earth
  A youth, to Fortune and to Fame unknown;
Fair Science frown'd not on his humble birth,
  And Melancholy mark'd him for her own.   120

Large was his bounty, and his soul sincere,
  Heaven did a' recompense as largely send;
He gave to Misery all he had, a tear;
  He gain'd from Heaven ('twas all he wish'd) a friend.

No farther seek his merits to disclose,   125
  Or draw his frailties from their dread abode,
(There they alike in trembling hope repose)
  The bosom of his Father and his God.

MISCELLANEOUS POEMS.

ON THE SPRING.

Lo! where the rosy-bosom'd Hours,
  Fair Venus' train, appear,
Disclose the long-expecting flowers,
  And wake the purple year!
The Attic warbler pours her throat,   5
  Responsive to the cuckoo's note,

The untaught harmony of spring ;
While, whispering pleasure as they fly,
Cool Zephyrs thro' the clear blue sky
　　Their gather'd fragrance fling.   10

Where'er the oak's thick branches stretch
　　A broader browner shade,
Where'er the rude and moss-grown beech
　　O'ercanopies the glade,
Beside some water's rushy brink   15
With me the Muse shall sit, and think
　　(At ease reclin'd in rustic state)
How vain the ardour of the crowd,
How low, how little are the proud,
　　How indigent the great !   20

Still is the toiling hand of Care ;
　　The panting herds repose :
Yet hark, how thro' the peopled air
　　The busy murmur glows !
The insect youth are on the wing,   25
Eager to taste the honied spring,
　　And float amid the liquid noon :
Some lightly o'er the current skim,
Some show their gayly-gilded trim
　　Quick-glancing to the sun.   30

To Contemplation's sober eye
　　Such is the race of Man ;
And they that creep, and they that fly,
　　Shall end where they began.

Alike the busy and the gay   35
But flutter thro' life's little day,
   In Fortune's varying colours drest :
Brush'd by the hand of rough Mischance,
Or chill'd by age, their airy dance
   They leave, in dust to rest.   40

Methinks I hear in accents low
   The sportive kind reply :
Poor moralist ! and what art thou?
   A solitary fly !
Thy joys no glittering female meets,   45
No hive hast thou of hoarded sweets,
   No painted plumage to display :
On hasty wings thy youth is flown ;
Thy sun is set, thy spring is gone—
   We frolic while 'tis May.   50

ON THE

DEATH OF A FAVOURITE CAT,

Drowned in a Tub of Gold Fishes.

'Twas on a lofty vase's side,
Where China's gayest art had dyed
   The azure flowers that blow;
Demurest of the tabby kind,
The pensive Selima, reclin'd,   5
   Gaz'd on the lake below.

Her conscious tail her joy declar'd :
The fair round face, the snowy beard,
   The velvet of her paws,
Her coat, that with the tortoise vies,   10
Her ears of jet, and emerald eyes,
   She saw; and purr'd applause.

Still had she gaz'd ; but midst the tide
Two angel forms were seen to glide,
   The Genii of the stream :   15
Their scaly armour's Tyrian hue
Through richest purple to the view
   Betray'd a golden gleam.

·The hapless nymph with wonder saw :
A whisker first, and then a claw,   20
   With many an ardent wish,
She stretch'd in vain to reach the prize.
What female heart can gold despise?
   What Cat's averse to fish?

Presumptuous maid ! with looks intent   25
Again she stretch'd, again she bent,
   Nor knew the gulf between.
(Malignant Fate sat by, and smil'd.)
The slippery verge her feet beguil'd,
   She tumbled headlong in.   30

Eight times emerging from the flood,
She mew'd to every watery God,
   Some speedy aid to send.
No Dolphin came, no Nereid stirr'd :
Nor cruel Tom, nor Susan heard.   35
   A favourite has no friend !

From hence, ye beauties, undeceiv'd,
Know, one false step is ne'er retriev'd,
   And be with caution bold.
Not all that tempts your wandering eyes   40
And heedless hearts is lawful prize,
   Nor all that glisters gold.
        D

ON A DISTANT
PROSPECT OF ETON COLLEGE.

Ἄνθρωπος, ἱκανὴ πρόφασις εἰς τὸ δυστυχεῖν.—MENANDER.

YE distant spires, ye antique towers,
    That crown the watery glade,
Where grateful Science still adores
    Her Henry's holy shade;

And ye, that from the stately brow   5
Of Windsor's heights th' expanse below
   Of grove, of lawn, of mead survey,
Whose turf, whose shade, whose flowers among
Wanders the hoary Thames along
   His silver-winding way :   10

Ah, happy hills ! ah, pleasing shade !
   Ah, fields belov'd in vain !
Where once my careless childhood stray'd,
   A stranger yet to pain !
I feel the gales that from ye blow   15
A momentary bliss bestow,
   As, waving fresh their gladsome wing,
My weary soul they seem to soothe,
And, redolent of joy and youth,
   To breathe a second spring.   20

Say, Father Thames, for thou hast seen
   Full many a sprightly race
Disporting on thy margent green
   The paths of pleasure trace ;
Who foremost now delight to cleave   25
With pliant arm thy glassy wave ?
   The captive linnet which enthrall ?
What idle progeny succeed
To chase the rolling circle's speed,
   Or urge the flying ball ?   30

While some, on earnest business bent,
   Their murmuring labours ply
'Gainst graver hours that bring constraint
   To sweeten liberty,

Some bold adventurers disdain   35
The limits of their little reign,
   And unknown regions dare descry :
Still as they run they look behind,
They hear a voice in every wind,
   And snatch a fearful joy.   40

Gay hope is theirs by fancy fed,
   Less pleasing when possest ;
The tear forgot as soon as shed,
   The sunshine of the breast :
Theirs buxom health of rosy hue,   45
Wild wit, invention ever new,
   And lively cheer of vigour born ;
The thoughtless day, the easy night,
The spirits pure, the slumbers light,
   That fly th' approach of morn.   50

Alas ! regardless of their doom,
   The little victims play ;
No sense have they of ills to come,
   No care beyond to-day :
Yet see how all around 'em wait   55
The ministers of human fate,
   And black Misfortune's baleful train !
Ah, show them where in ambush stand
To seize their prey the murtherous band !
   Ah, tell them, they are men !   60

These shall the fury Passions tear,
   The vultures of the mind,
Disdainful Anger, pallid Fear,
   And Shame that skulks behind ;

Or pining Love shall waste their youth,   65
Or Jealousy with rankling tooth,
   That inly gnaws the secret heart;
And Envy wan, and faded Care,
Grim-visag'd comfortless Despair,
   And Sorrow's piercing dart.   70

Ambition this shall tempt to rise,
   Then whirl the wretch from high,
To bitter Scorn a sacrifice,
   And grinning Infamy.
The stings of Falsehood those shall try,   75
And hard Unkindness' alter'd eye,
   That mocks the tear it forc'd to flow;'
And keen Remorse with blood defil'd,
And moody Madness laughing wild
   Amid severest woe.   80

Lo! in the vale of years beneath
   A grisly troop are seen,
The painful family of Death,
   More hideous than their queen:
This racks the joints, this fires the veins,   85
That every labouring sinew strains,
   Those in the deeper vitals rage:
Lo! Poverty, to fill the band,
That numbs the soul with icy hand,
   And slow-consuming Age.   90

To each his sufferings: all are men,
   Condemn'd alike to groan;
The tender for another's pain,
   Th' unfeeling for his own.

Yet, ah! why should they know their fate,   95
Since sorrow never comes too late,
   And happiness too swiftly flies?
Thought would destroy their paradise.
No more;—where ignorance is bliss,
   'Tis folly to be wise.   100

APOLLO CITHARŒDUS.   FROM THE VATICAN.

THE PROGRESS OF POESY.

A Pindaric Ode.

Φωνᾶντα συνετοῖσιν· ἐς
Δὲ τὸ πᾶν ἑρμηνέων
Χατίζει.—PINDAR, *Ol.* II.

I. I.

AWAKE, Æolian lyre, awake,
And give to rapture all thy trembling strings.
From Helicon's harmonious springs
   A thousand rills their mazy progress take :
The laughing flowers that round them blow,   5
Drink life and fragrance as they flow.
Now the rich stream of music winds along,
Deep, majestic, smooth, and strong,
Thro' verdant vales, and Ceres' golden reign :
Now rolling down the steep amain,   10
Headlong, impetuous, see it pour ;
The rocks and nodding groves rebellow to the roar.

I. 2.

Oh! Sovereign of the willing soul,
Parent of sweet and solemn-breathing airs,
Enchanting shell! the sullen Cares   15
     And frantic Passions hear thy soft control.
On Thracia's hills the Lord of War
Has curb'd the fury of his car,
And dropt his thirsty lance at thy command.
Perching on the sceptred hand   20
Of Jove, thy magic lulls the feather'd king
With ruffled plumes and flagging wing:
Quench'd in dark clouds of slumber lie
The terror of his beak, and lightnings of his eye.

I. 3.

Thee the voice, the dance, obey,   25
Temper'd to thy warbled lay.
O'er Idalia's velvet-green
The rosy-crowned Loves are seen
On Cytherea's day
With antic Sports, and blue-eyed Pleasures,   30
Frisking light in frolic measures;
Now pursuing, now retreating,
     Now in circling troops they meet:
To brisk notes in cadence beating,
     Glance their many-twinkling feet.   35
Slow melting strains their Queen's approach declare:
     Where'er she turns the Graces homage pay.
With arms sublime, that float upon the air,
     In gliding state she wins her easy way:
O'er her warm cheek, and rising bosom, move   40
The bloom of young Desire and purple light of Love.

II. I.

Man's feeble race what ills await!
Labour, and Penury, the racks of Pain,
Disease, and Sorrow's weeping train,
 And Death, sad refuge from the storms of Fate!   45
The fond complaint, my song, disprove,
And justify the laws of Jove.
Say, has he given in vain the heavenly Muse?
Night and all her sickly dews,
Her spectres wan, and birds of boding cry,   50
He gives to range the dreary sky;
Till down the eastern cliffs afar
Hyperion's march they spy, and glittering shafts of war.

II. 2.

In climes beyond the solar road,
Where shaggy forms o'er ice-built mountains roam, 55
The Muse has broke the twilight gloom
 To cheer the shivering native's dull abode.
And oft, beneath the odorous shade
Of Chili's boundless forests laid,
She deigns to hear the savage youth repeat,   60
In loose numbers wildly sweet,
Their feather-cinctur'd chiefs, and dusky loves.
Her track, where'er the Goddess roves,
Glory pursue, and generous Shame,
Th' unconquerable Mind, and Freedom's holy flame. 65

II. 3.

Woods, that wave o'er Delphi's steep,
Isles, that crown th' Ægean deep,

DELPHI AND MOUNT PARNASSUS.

Fields, that cool Ilissus laves,
Or where Mæander's amber waves
In lingering labyrinths creep, 70
How do your tuneful echoes languish,
Mute, but to the voice of anguish!
Where each old poetic mountain
  Inspiration breath'd around;
Every shade and hallow'd fountain 75
  Murmur'd deep a solemn sound:
Till the sad Nine, in Greece's evil hour,
  Left their Parnassus for the Latian plains.
Alike they scorn the pomp of tyrant Power,
  And coward Vice, that revels in her chains. 80
When Latium had her lofty spirit lost,
They sought, O Albion! next thy sea-encircled coast.

III. I.

Far from the sun and summer gale,
In thy green lap was Nature's darling laid,
  What time, where lucid Avon stray'd,   85
    To him the mighty mother did unveil
Her awful face : the dauntless child
Stretch'd forth his little arms and smil'd.
"This pencil take (she said), whose colours clear
Richly paint the vernal year :   90
Thine too these golden keys, immortal Boy !
This can unlock the gates of joy;
Of horror that, and thrilling fears,
Or ope the sacred source of sympathetic tears."

THE AVON AND STRATFORD CHURCH.

III. 2.

Nor second He, that rode sublime 　　　　　　　　95
Upon the seraph wings of Ecstasy,
The secrets of th' abyss to spy.
　　He pass'd the flaming bounds of place and time:
The living throne, the sapphire blaze,
Where angels tremble while they gaze, 　　　　　　100
He saw; but, blasted with excess of light,
Clos'd his eyes in endless night.
Behold, where Dryden's less presumptuous car,
Wide o'er the fields of glory bear
Two coursers of ethereal race, 　　　　　　　　105
With necks in thunder cloth'd, and long-resounding pace.

III. 3.

Hark, his hands the lyre explore!
Bright-eyed Fancy hovering o'er
Scatters from her pictur'd urn
Thoughts that breathe, and words that burn. 　　　　110
But ah! 'tis heard no more——
Oh! lyre divine, what daring spirit
Wakes thee now? Tho' he inherit
Nor the pride, nor ample pinion,
　　That the Theban eagle bear, 　　　　　　　115
Sailing with supreme dominion
　　Thro' the azure deep of air,
Yet oft before his infant eyes would run
　　Such forms as glitter in the Muse's ray
With orient hues, unborrow'd of the sun: 　　　　120
　　Yet shall he mount, and keep his distant way
Beyond the limits of a vulgar fate,
Beneath the Good how far—but far above the Great.

THE BARD.

A Pindaric Ode.

I. I.

" RUIN seize thee, ruthless King !
   Confusion on thy banners wait ;
Tho' fann'd by Conquest's crimson wing,
   They mock the air with idle state.
Helm, nor hauberk's twisted mail,
Nor e'en thy virtues, Tyrant, shall avail

To save thy secret soul from nightly fears,
From Cambria's curse, from Cambria's tears!"
   Such were the sounds that o'er the crested pride
Of the first Edward scatter'd wild dismay,   10
   As down the steep of Snowdon's shaggy side
He wound with toilsome march his long array.
Stout Gloster stood aghast in speechless trance:
" To arms!" cried Mortimer, and couch'd his quivering
     lance.

I. 2.

   On a rock whose haughty brow   15
Frowns o'er old Conway's foaming flood,
   Rob'd in the sable garb of woe,
With haggard eyes the poet stood
(Loose his beard, and hoary hair
Stream'd, like a meteor, to the troubled air),   20
And with a master's hand, and prophet's fire,
Struck the deep sorrows of his lyre.
" Hark, how each giant oak, and desert cave,
   Sighs to the torrent's awful voice beneath!
O'er thee, O King! their hundred arms they wave,   25
   Revenge on thee in hoarser murmurs breathe;
Vocal no more, since Cambria's fatal day,
To high-born Hoel's harp, or soft Llewellyn's lay.

I. 3.

   " Cold is Cadwallo's tongue,
   That hush'd the stormy main;   30
Brave Urien sleeps upon his craggy bed;
   Mountains, ye mourn in vain
   Modred, whose magic song
Made huge Plinlimmon bow his cloud-topt head.

On dreary Arvon's shore they lie, 35
Smear'd with gore, and ghastly pale :
Far, far aloof th' affrighted ravens sail ;   •
 The famish'd eagle screams, and passes by.
Dear lost companions of my tuneful art,
 Dear as the light that visits these sad eyes, 40
Dear as the ruddy drops that warm my heart,
 Ye died amidst your dying country's cries—
No more I weep. They do not sleep.
 On yonder cliffs, a grisly band,
I see them sit, they linger yet, 45
 Avengers of their native land :
With me in dreadful harmony they join,
And weave with bloody hands the tissue of thy line.

II. 1.

"Weave the warp, and weave the woof,
 The winding-sheet of Edward's race. 50
Give ample room, and verge enough
 The characters of hell to trace.
Mark the year, and mark the night,
When Severn shall reëcho with affright
The shrieks of death thro' Berkeley's roofs that ring, 55
Shrieks of an agonizing king !
 She-wolf of France, with unrelenting fangs,
That tear'st the bowels of thy mangled mate,
 From thee be born, who o'er thy country hangs
The scourge of heaven. What terrors round him wait ! 60
Amazement in his van, with Flight combin'd,
And Sorrow's faded form, and Solitude behind.

II. 2.

"Mighty victor, mighty lord !
Low on his funeral couch he lies !

No pitying heart, no eye, afford   65
A tear to grace his obsequies.
Is the sable.warrior fled?
Thy son is gone.   He rests among the dead.
The swarm that in thy noontide beam were born ? .
Gone to salute the rising morn.   70
Fair laughs the morn, and soft the zephyr blows,
   While proudly riding o'er the azure realm
In gallant trim the gilded vessel goes;
   Youth on the prow, and Pleasure at the helm;
Regardless of the sweeping whirlwind's sway,   75
That, hush'd in grim repose, expects his evening prey.

II. 3.

  "Fill high the sparkling bowl,
   The rich repast prepare;
Reft of a crown, he yet may share the feast:
   Close by the regal chair   80
   Fell Thirst and Famine scowl
A baleful smile upon their baffled guest.
   Heard ye the din of battle bray,
Lance to lance, and horse to horse?
Long years of havoc urge their destined course,   85
   And thro' the kindred squadrons mow their way.
Ye towers of Julius, London's lasting shame,
   With many a foul and midnight murther fed,
Revere his consort's faith, his father's fame,
   And spare the meek usurper's holy head.   90
Above, below, the rose of snow,
   Twin'd with her blushing foe, we spread:
The bristled boar in infant gore
   Wallows beneath the thorny shade.
Now, brothers, bending o'er the accursed loom,   95
Stamp we our vengeance deep, and ratify his doom.

THE BLOODY TOWER.

III. I.

" Edward, lo ! to sudden fate
   (Weave we the woof.   The thread is spun.)
Half of thy heart we consecrate.
   (The web is wove.   The work is done.)   100
Stay, oh stay ! nor thus forlorn
Leave me unbless'd, unpitied, here to mourn :
In yon bright track, that fires the western skies,
They melt, they vanish from my eyes.

E

But oh! what solemn scenes on Snowdon's height   105
Descending slow their glittering skirts unroll?
   Visions of glory, spare my aching sight!
Ye unborn ages, crowd not on my soul!
No more our long-lost Arthur we bewail.
All hail, ye genuine kings, Britannia's issue, hail!   110

III. 2.

   " Girt with many a baron bold
Sublime their starry fronts they rear;
   And gorgeous dames, and statesmen old
In bearded majesty, appear.
In the midst a form divine!   115
Her eye proclaims her of the Briton line;
Her lion-port, her awe-commanding face,
Attemper'd sweet to virgin-grace.
What strings symphonious tremble in the air,
   What strains of vocal transport round her play!   120
Hear from the grave, great Taliessin, hear;
   They breathe a soul to animate thy clay.
Bright Rapture calls, and soaring as she sings,
Waves in the eye of heaven her many-colour'd wings.

III. 3.

   "The verse adorn again   125
   Fierce War, and faithful Love,
And Truth severe, by fairy Fiction drest.
   In buskin'd measures move
   Pale Grief, and pleasing Pain,
With Horror, tyrant of the throbbing breast.   130
   A voice, as of the cherub-choir,
Gales from blooming Eden bear;
And distant warblings lessen on my ear,
   That lost in long futurity expire.

Fond impious man, think'st thou yon sanguine cloud, 135
   Rais'd by thy breath, has quench'd the orb of day?
To-morrow he repairs the golden flood,
   And warms the nations with redoubled ray.
Enough for me; with joy I see
   The different doom our fates assign. 140
Be thine despair, and sceptred care;
   To triumph, and to die, are mine."
He spoke, and headlong from the mountain's height
Deep in the roaring tide he plung'd to endless night.

QUEEN ELIZABETH.

HYMN TO ADVERSITY.

Ζῆνα ——————
Τὸν φρονεῖν βροτοὺς ὁδώ-
σαντα, τῷ πάθει μαθὰν
Θέντα κυρίως ἔχειν.
    ÆSCHYLUS, *Agam.*

DAUGHTER of Jove, relentless power,
    Thou tamer of the human breast,
Whose iron scourge and torturing hour
    The bad affright, afflict the best!
Bound in thy adamantine chain,   5
The proud are taught to taste of pain,
And purple tyrants vainly groan
With pangs unfelt before, unpitied and alone.

When first thy sire to send on earth
    Virtue, his darling child, design'd,   10
To thee he gave the heavenly birth,
    And bade to form her infant mind.
Stern rugged nurse! thy rigid lore
With patience many a year she bore:
What sorrow was, thou bad'st her know,   15
And from her own she learn'd to melt at others' woe.

Scar'd at thy frown terrific, fly
    Self-pleasing Folly's idle brood,
Wild Laughter, Noise, and thoughtless Joy,
    And leave us leisure to be good.   20
Light they disperse, and with them go
The summer friend, the flattering foe ;
By vain Prosperity receiv'd,
To her they vow their truth, and are again believ'd.

Wisdom in sable garb array'd,   25
    Immersed in rapturous thought profound,
And Melancholy, silent maid,
    With leaden eye that loves the ground,
Still on thy solemn steps attend ;
Warm Charity, the general friend,   30
With Justice, to herself severe,
And Pity, dropping soft the sadly-pleasing tear.

Oh! gently on thy suppliant's head,
    Dread goddess, lay thy chastening hand !
Not in thy Gorgon terrors clad,   35
    Not circled with the vengeful band
(As by the impious thou art seen),
With thundering voice and threatening mien,
With screaming Horror's funeral cry,
Despair, and fell Disease, and ghastly Poverty :   40

Thy form benign, O goddess, wear,
    Thy milder influence impart ;
Thy philosophic train be there
    To soften, not to wound, my heart.
The generous spark extinct revive,   45
Teach me to love and to forgive, .
Exact my own defects to scan,
What others are to feel, and know myself a Man.

BERKELEY CASTLE.

"Mark the year, and mark the night,
  When Severn shall reëcho with affright
  The shrieks of death thro' Berkeley's roofs that ring,
  Shrieks of an agonizing king!"
                              The Bard, 53.

NOTES.

LIST OF ABBREVIATIONS.

A. S., Anglo-Saxon.
Arc., Milton's *Arcades.*
C. T., Chaucer's *Canterbury Tales.*
Cf. (*confer*), compare.
D. V., Goldsmith's *Deserted Village.*
Ep., Epistle, Epode.
Foll., following.
F. Q., Spenser's *Faërie Queene.,*
H., Haven's *Rhetoric* (Harper's edition).
Hales, *Longer English Poems,* edited by Rev. J. W. Hales (London, 1872).
Il Pens., Milton's *Il Penseroso.*
L'All.,   "   *L'Allegro.*
Ol., Pindar's *Olympian Odes.*
P. L., Milton's *Paradise Lost.*
P. R.,   "   "   *Regained.*
S. A.,   "   *Samson Agonistes.*
Shakes. Gr., Abbott's *Shakespearian Grammar* (the references are to *sections,* not pages).
Shep. Kal., Spenser's *Shepherd's Kalendar.*
st., stanza.
Wb., Webster's Dictionary (last revised quarto edition).
Worc., Worcester's Dictionary (quarto edition).

Other abbreviations (names of books in the Bible, plays of Shakespeare, works of Ovid, Virgil, and Horace, etc.) need no explanation.

NOTES.

: Curfew tolls the Knell of parting Day,
lowing Herd wind slowly o'er the Lea,
Plowman homeward plods his weary Way.
) leaves the World to Darkness & to me.

No farther seek his Merits to disclose,
; draw his Frailties from their dread Abode,
ere they alike in trembling Hope repose)
: Bosom of his Father, & his God.

ELEGY IN A COUNTRY CHURCHYARD.

This poem was begun in the year 1742, but was not finished until 1750, when Gray sent it to Walpole with a letter (dated June 12, 1750) in which he says: "I have been here at Stoke a few days (where I shall continue good part of the summer), and having put an end to a thing, whose beginning you have seen long ago, I immediately send it you. You will, I hope, look upon it in the light of a thing with an end to it: a merit that most of my writings have wanted, and are like to want." It was shown in manuscript to some of the author's friends, and was published in 1751 only because it was about to be printed surreptitiously.

February 11, 1751, Gray wrote to Walpole that the proprietors of "the Magazine of Magazines" were about to publish his _Elegy_, and added, "I have but one bad way left to escape the honour they would inflict upon me; and therefore am obliged to desire you would make Dodsley print it immediately (which may be done in less than a week's time) from your copy, but without my name, in what form is most convenient for him, but on his best paper and character; he must correct the press himself,*

---

* Dodsley's proof-reading must have been somewhat careless, for there are many errors of the press in this _editio princeps_. Gray writes to Walpole, under date of "Ash-Wednesday, Cambridge, 1751," as follows: "Nurse Dodsley has given it a

and print it without any interval between the stanzas, because the sense
is in some places continued beyond them ; and the title must be—' Elegy,
written in a Country Churchyard.' If he would add a line or two to say
it came into his hands by accident, I should like it better." Walpole
did as requested, and wrote an advertisement to the effect that accident
alone brought the poem before the public, although an apology was un-
necessary to any but the author. On which Gray wrote, " I thank you
for your advertisement, which saves my honour."

A writer in *Notes and Queries*, June 12, 1875, states that the poem first
appeared in the *London Magazine*, March, 1751, p. 134, and that "the
Magazine of Magazines" is "a gentle term of scorn used by Gray to indi-
cate " that periodical, and not the name of any actual magazine. But in
the next number of *Notes and Queries* (June 19, 1875) Mr. F. Locker
informs us that he has in his possession a title-page of the *Grand Magazine of Magazines*, and the page of the number for April, 1751, which
contains the *Elegy*. The magazine is said to be "collected and digested
by Roger Woodville, Esq.," and "published by Cooper at the Globe, in
Pater Noster Row."

Gray says nothing in his letters of the appearance of the *Elegy* in the
London Magazine. The full title of that periodical was "The London
Magazine : or Gentleman's Monthly Intelligencer." The editor's name
was not given; the publisher was "R. Baldwin, jun. at the Rose in Pater-
Noster Row." The volume for 1751 was the 20th, and the Preface (written at the close of the year) begins thus : "As the two most formidable
Enemies we have ever had, are now extinct, we have great Reason to
conclude, that it is only the Merit, and real Usefulness of our COLLEC-
TION, that hath supported its Sale and Reputation for Twenty Years."
A foot-note informs us that the " Enemies " are the " *Magazine of Magazines* and *Grand Magazine of Magazines ;*" from which it would appear
that there were two periodicals of similar name published in London in
1751.*

---

pinch or two in the cradle, that (I doubt) it will bear the marks of as long as it lives.
But no matter: we have ourselves suffered under her hands before now; and besides,
it will only look the more careless and by *accident* as it were." Again, March 3, 1751,
he writes: "I do not expect any more editions; as I have appeared in more magazines
than one. The chief errata were *sacred* for *secret ; hidden* for *kindred* (in spite of
dukes and classics); and '*frowning* as in scorn' for *smiling*. I humbly propose, for
the benefit of Mr. Dodsley and his matrons, that take *awake* [in line 92, which at first
read "awake and faithful to her wonted fires"] for a verb, that they should read *asleep*,
and all will be right." Other errors were, "Their *harrow* oft the stubborn glebe,"
"And read their *destiny* in a nation's eyes," "With uncouth rhymes and shapeless
culture decked," "Slow through the churchway *pass*," and many of minor importance.

* May not the *Elegy* have been printed in both of these? We do not know how
otherwise to reconcile the conflicting statements concerning the "Magazine of Magazines," as Gray calls it. In the first place, Gray appears (from other portions of his
letter to Walpole) to be familiar with this magazine, and would not be likely to confound
it with another of similar name. Then, as we have seen, he writes *early in March* to
Walpole that the poem has been printed "in more magazines than one." This cannot refer to the *Grand Magazine of Magazines*, if, as Mr. Locker states, it was the
April number of that periodical in which the poem appeared. Nor can it refer to the
London Magazine, as it is clear from internal evidence that the March number, containing the *Elegy*, was not issued until early in April. It contains a summary of current
news down to Sunday, March 31, and the price of stocks in the London market for

The author's name is not given with the *Elegy* as printed in the *London Magazine.* The poem is sandwiched between an "Epilogue to *Alfred, a Masque*" and some coarse rhymes entitled "Strip-Me-Naked, or Royal Gin for ever." There is not even a printer's "rule" or "dash" to separate the title of the latter from the last line of the *Elegy.* The poem is more correctly printed than in Dodsley's authorized edition; though, queerly enough, it has "winds" in the second line and the parenthesis "(all he had)" in the Epitaph. Of Dodsley's misprints noted above it has only "Their *harrow* oft" and "shapeless *culture.*" These four errors, indeed, are the only ones worth noting, except "Or *wake* to extasy the living lyre."

The "Magazine of Magazines" (as the writer in the *North American Review* tells us) printed the *Elegy* with the author's name. The authorized though anonymous edition was thus briefly nóticed by *The Monthly Review*, the critical Rhadamanthus of the day : "*An Elegy in a Country Churchyard.* 4to. Dodsley's. Seven pages.—The excellence of this little piece amply compensates for its want of quantity."

"Soon after its publication," says Mason, "I remember, sitting with Mr. Gray in his College apartment, he expressed to me his surprise at the rapidity of its sale. I replied :

> 'Sunt lacrymae rerum, et mentem mortalia tangunt.'

He paused awhile, and taking his pen, wrote the line on a printed copy of it lying on his table. 'This,' said he, 'shall be its future motto.' 'Pity,' cried I, 'that Dr. Young's Night Thoughts have preoccupied it.' 'So,' replied he, 'indeed it is.'" Gray himself tells the story of its success on the margin of the manuscript copy of the *Elegy* preserved at Cambridge among his papers, and reproduced in *fac-simile* in Mathias's elegant edition of the poet. The following is a careful transcript of the memorandum :

"publish'd in | **Feb:**^{ry}. 1751. | by Dodsley: & | went thro' four | Editions ; in two | months; and af- | terwards a fifth | 6th 7th & 8th 9th & 10th | & 11th | printed also in 1753 | with Mr Bentley's | Designs, of w^{ch} | there is a 2^d Edition | & again by **Dodsley** | in his Miscellany, | Vol :

March 30. The *February* number, in its "monthly catalogue" of new books, records the publication of the *Elegy* by Dodsley thus : "An Elegy wrote in a Church-yard, pr. 6d. Dodsley."

If, then, the *Elegy* did not appear in either the *London Magazine* or the *Grand Magazine of Magazines* until more than a month (in the case of the latter, perhaps two months) after Dodsley had issued it, in what magazine was it that it *did* appear just before he issued it? The *N. A. Review* says that "it was a close race between the Magazine and Dodsley ; but the former, having a little the start, came out a few days ahead." If so, it must have been the *March* number ; or the *February* one, if it was published, like the *London*, at the end of the month. Gray calls it "the Magazine of Magazines," and we shall take his word for it until we have reason for doubting it. What else was included in his "more magazines than one" we cannot even guess.

We have not been able to find the *Magazine of Magazines* or the *Grand Magazine of Magazines* in the libraries, and know nothing about either "of our own knowledge." The *London Magazine* is in the Harvard College Library, and the statements concerning that we can personally vouch for.

4th & in a | Scotch Collection | call'd *the Union.* | translated into | Latin by Chr : Anstey | Esq, & the Revd Mr | Roberts, & publish'd | in 1762 ; & again | in the same year | by Rob : Lloyd, M : A :"

"One peculiar and remarkable tribute to the merit of the *Elegy,*" says Professor Henry Reed, "is to be noticed in the great number of translations which have been made of it into various languages, both of ancient and modern Europe. It is the same kind of tribute which has been rendered to *Robinson Crusoe* and to *The Pilgrim's Progress,* and is proof of the same universality of interest, transcending the limits of language and of race. To no poem in the English language has the same kind of homage been paid so abundantly. Of what other poem is there a polyglot edition? Italy and England have competed with their polyglot editions of the *Elegy:* Torri's, bearing the title, ' Elegia di Tomaso Gray sopra un Cimitero di Campagna, tradotta dall' Inglese in più lingue : Verona, 1817; Livorno, 1843 ;' and Van Voorst's London edition." Professor Reed adds a list of the translations (which, however, is incomplete), including one in Hebrew, seven in Greek, twelve in Latin, thirteen in Italian, fifteen in French, six in German, and one in Portuguese.

"Had Gray written nothing but his *Elegy,*" remarks Byron, "high as he stands, I am not sure that he would not stand higher ; it is the cornerstone of his glory."

The tribute paid the poem by General Wolfe is familiar to all, but we cannot refrain from quoting Lord Mahon's beautiful account of it in his *History of England.* On the night of September 13th, 1759, the night before the battle on the Plains of Abraham, Wolfe was descending the St. Lawrence with a part of his troops. The historian says : "Swiftly, but silently, did the boats fall down with the tide, unobserved by the enemy's sentinels at their posts along the shore. Of the soldiers on board, how eagerly must every heart have throbbed at the coming conflict ! how intently must every eye have contemplated the dark outline, as it lay pencilled upon the midnight sky, and as every moment it grew closer and clearer, of the hostile heights ! Not a word was spoken—not a sound heard beyond the rippling of the stream. Wolfe alone—thus tradition has told us—repeated in a low tone to the other officers in his boat those beautiful stanzas with which a country churchyard inspired the muse of Gray. One noble line,

> ' The paths of glory lead but to the grave,'

must have seemed at such a moment fraught with mournful meaning. At the close of the recitation Wolfe added, ' Now, gentlemen, I would rather be the author of that poem than take Quebec.' "

Hales, in his Introduction to the poem, remarks : " The *Elegy* is perhaps the most widely known poem in our language. The reason of this extensive popularity is perhaps to be sought in the fact that it expresses in an exquisite manner feelings and thoughts that are universal. In the current of ideas in the *Elegy* there is perhaps nothing that is rare, or exceptional, or out of the common way. The musings are of the most rational and obvious character possible ; it is difficult to conceive of any one musing under similar circumstances who should not muse so ; but they are not the less deep and moving on this account. The mystery of life does not become clearer, or less solemn and awful, for any amount of contemplation. Such inevitable, such everlasting questions as rise on the mind when one lingers in the precincts of Death can never lose their freshness, never cease to fascinate and to move. It is with such questions, that would have been commonplace long ages since if they could ever be so, that the *Elegy* deals. It deals with them in no lofty philosophical manner, but in a simple, humble, unpretentious way, always with the truest and the broadest humanity. The poet's thoughts turn to the poor ; he forgets the fine tombs inside the church, and thinks only of the 'mouldering heaps' in the churchyard. Hence the problem that especially suggests itself is the potential greatness, when they lived, of the 'rude forefathers' that now lie at his feet. He does not, and cannot solve it, though he finds considerations to mitigate the sadness it must inspire ; but he expresses it in all its awfulness in the most effective language and with the deepest feeling ; and his expression of it has become a living part of our language."

The writer in the *North American Review* (vol. 96) from whom we have elsewhere quoted says of the *Elegy :* "It is upon this that Gray's fame as a poet must chiefly rest. By this he will be known forever alike to the lettered and the unlettered. Many, in future ages, who may never have heard of his classic Odes, his various learning, or his sparkling letters, will revere him only as the author of the *Elegy.* For this he will be enshrined through all time in the hearts of the myriads who shall speak our English tongue. For this his name will be held in glad remembrance in the far-off summer isles of the Pacific, and amidst the waste of polar snows. If he had written nothing else, his place as a leading poet in our language would still be assured. Many have asserted, with Johnson, that he was a mere mechanical poet—one who brought from without, but never found within ; that the gift of inspiration was not native to him ; that his imagination was borrowed finery, his fancy tinsel, and his invention the world's well-worn jewels ; that whatever in his verse was poetic was not new, and what was new was not poetic ; that he was only an unworldly dyspeptic, living amid many books, and laboriously delving for a lifetime between musty covers, picking out now and then another's gems and bits of ore, and fashioning them into ill-compacted mosaics, which he wrongly called his own. To all this the *Elegy* is a sufficient answer. It is not old—it is not bookish ; it is new and human. Books could not make its maker : he was born of the divine breath alone. Consider all the commentators, the scholiasts, the interpreters, the annotators, and other like book-worms, from Aristarchus down to Döderlein ; and may it not be said that, among them all, 'Nec viget quidquam simile aut secundum ?'

"Gray wrote but little, yet he wrote that little well. He might have done far more for us ; the same is true of most men, even of the greatest. The possibilities of a life are always in advance of its performance. But we cannot say that his life was a wasted one. Even this little *Elegy* alone should go for much. For, suppose that he had never written this, but instead had done much else in other ways, according to his powers :

that he had written many learned treatises ; that he had, with keen criticism, expounded and reconstructed Greek classics ; that he had, perchance, sat upon the woolsack, and laid rich offerings at the feet of blind
Justice ;—taking the years together, would it have been, on the whole,
better for him or for us ? Would he have added so much to the sum of
human happiness ? He might thus have made himself a power for a
time, to be dethroned by some new usurper in the realm of knowledge ;
now he is a power and a joy forever to countless thousands."

Two manuscripts of the *Elegy*, in Gray's handwriting, still exist. Both
were bequeathed by the poet, together with his library, letters, and many
miscellaneous papers, to his friends the Rev. William Mason and the Rev.
James Browne, as joint literary executors. Mason bequeathed the entire
trust to Mr. Stonhewer. The latter, in making his will, divided the legacy
into two parts. The larger share went to the Master and Fellows of
Pembroke Hall. Among the papers, which are still in the possession of
the College, was found a copy of the *Elegy*. An excellent fac-simile of
this manuscript appears in Mathias's edition of Gray, published in 1814.
In referring to it hereafter we shall designate it as the " Pembroke " MS.
The remaining portion of Gray's literary bequest, including the other
manuscript of the *Elegy*, was left by Mr. Stonhewer to his friend, Mr.
Bright. In 1845 Mr. Bright's sons sold the collection at auction. The
MS. of the *Elegy* was bought by Mr. Granville John Penn, of Stoke Park,
for *one hundred pounds*—the highest sum that had ever been known to
be paid for a single sheet of paper. In 1854 this manuscript came again
into the market, and was knocked down to Mr. Robert Charles Wrightson, of Birmingham, for £131. On the 29th of May, 1875, it was once
more offered for sale in London, and was purchased by Sir William
Fraser for £230, or about $1150. A photographic reproduction of it
was published in London in 1862. For convenience we shall refer to it
as the " Wrightson " MS.
There can be little doubt that the Wrightson MS. is the original one,
and that the Pembroke MS. is a fair copy made from it by the poet. The
former contains a greater number of alterations, and varies more from the
printed text. It bears internal evidence of being the rough draft, while
the other represents a later stage of the poem. We will give the variations of both from the present version.*
The Wrightson MS. has in the first stanza, " The lowing herd *wind*
slowly," etc. See our note on this line, below.
In the 2d stanza, it reads, " And *now* the air," etc.
The 5th stanza is as follows :

---

* For the readings of the Wrightson MS. we have had to depend on Mason, Mitford,
and other editors of the poem, and on the article in the *North American Review,*
already referred to. The readings of the Pembroke MS. are taken from the engraved
fac-simile in Mathias's edition.
The two stanzas of which a fac-simile is given on page 73 are from the Pembroke
MS., but the wood-cut hardly does justice to the feminine delicacy of the poet's handwriting.

> "For ever sleep: the breezy call of morn,
> Or swallow twitt'ring from the straw-built shed,
> Or Chanticleer so shrill, or echoing horn,
> No more shall rouse them from their lowly bed."

In 8th stanza, "Their *rustic* joys," etc.
In 10th stanza, the first two lines read,

> "Forgive, ye proud, th' involuntary fault,
> If memory to these no trophies raise."

In 12th stanza, "Hands that the *reins* of empire," etc.
In 13th stanza, "Chill Penury *depress'd*," etc.
The 14th stanza reads thus:

> "Some village Cato, who, with dauntless breast,
> The little tyrant of his fields withstood;
> Some mute inglorious Tully here may rest,
> Some Cæsar guiltless of his country's blood."*

In 18th stanza, "Or *crown* the shrine," etc.
After this stanza, the MS. has the following four stanzas, now omitted:

> "The thoughtless world to Majesty may bow,
> Exalt the brave, and idolize success;
> But more to innocence their safety owe
> Than Pow'r, or Genius, e'er conspir'd to bless.

---

* The *Saturday Review* for June 19, 1875, has a long article on the change made by Gray in this stanza, entitled, "A Lesson from Gray's Elegy," from which we cull the following paragraphs:
"Gray, having first of all put down the names of three Romans as illustrations of his meaning, afterwards deliberately struck them out and put the names of three Englishmen instead. This is a sign of a change in the taste of the age, a change with which Gray himself had a good deal to do. The deliberate wiping out of the names of Cato, Tully, and Cæsar, to put in the names of Hampden, Milton, and Cromwell, seems to us so obviously a change for the better that there seems to be no room for any doubt about it. It is by no means certain that Gray's own contemporaries would have thought the matter equally clear. We suspect that to many people in his day it must have seemed a daring novelty to draw illustrations from English history, especially from parts of English history which, it must be remembered, were then a great deal more recent than they are now. To be sure, in choosing English illustrations, a poet of Gray's time was in rather a hard strait. If he chose illustrations from the century or two before his own time, he could only choose names which had hardly got free from the strife of recent politics. If, in a poem of the nature of the Elegy, he had drawn illustrations from earlier times of English history, he would have found but few people in his day likely to understand him. . . .
"The change which Gray made in this well-known stanza is not only an improvement in a particular poem, it is a sign of a general improvement in taste. He wrote first according to the vicious taste of an earlier time, and he then changed it according to his own better taste. And of that better taste he was undoubtedly a prophet to others. Gray's poetry must have done a great deal to open men's eyes to the fact that they were Englishmen, and that on them, as Englishmen, English things had a higher claim than Roman, and that to them English examples ought to be more speaking than Roman ones. But there is another side of the case not to be forgotten. Those who would have regretted the change from Cato, Tully, and Cæsar to Hampden, Milton, and Cromwell, those who perhaps really did think that the bringing in of Hampden, Milton, and Cromwell was a degradation of what they would have called the Muse, were certainly not those who had the truest knowledge of Cato, Tully, and Cæsar. The 'classic' taste from which Gray helped to deliver us was a taste which hardly deserves to be called a taste. Pardonable perhaps in the first heat of the Renaissance, when 'classic' studies and objects had the charm of novelty, it had become by his day a mere silly fashion."

> "And thou who, mindful of the unhonour'd Dead,
>   Dost in these notes their artless tale relate,
> By night and lonely contemplation led
>   To wander in the gloomy walks of fate:
>
> "Hark! how the sacred Calm, that breathes around,
>   Bids every fierce tumultuous passion cease;
> In still small accents whisp'ring from the ground
>   A grateful earnest of eternal peace.
>
> "No more, with reason and thyself at strife,
>   Give anxious cares and endless wishes room;
> But through the cool sequester'd vale of life
>   Pursue the silent tenor of thy doom."*

The second of these stanzas has been remodelled and used as the 24th of the present version. Mason thought that there was a pathetic melancholy in all four which claimed preservation. The third he considered equal to any in the whole *Elegy*. The poem was originally intended to end here, the introduction of "the hoary-headed swain" being a happy after-thought.

In the 19th stanza, the MS. has "never *learn'd* to stray."

In the 21st stanza, "fame and *epitaph*," etc.

In the 23d stanza, the last line reads,

> "And buried ashes glow with social fires."

"Social" subsequently became "wonted," and other changes were made (see p. 74, foot-note) before the line took its present form.

The 24th stanza reads,

> "If chance that e'er some pensive Spirit more,
>   By sympathetic musings here delay'd,
> With vain, though kind inquiry shall explore
>   Thy once-lov'd haunt, this long-deserted shade."†

The last line of the 25th stanza reads,

> "On the high brow of yonder hanging lawn."

Then comes the following stanza, afterwards omitted:

> "Him have we seen the greenwood side along,
>   While o'er the heath we hied, our labour done,
> Oft as the woodlark pip'd her farewell song,
>   With wistful eyes pursue the setting sun."‡

Mason remarked: "I rather wonder that he rejected this stanza, as it not only has the same sort of Doric delicacy which charms us peculiarly

---

* We follow Mason (ed. 1778) in the text of these stanzas. The *North American Review* has "Power *and* Genius" in the first, and "*linger* in the *lonely* walks" in the second.

† Mitford (Eton ed.) gives "sympathizing" in the second line, and for the last,

> "Thy ever loved haunt—this long deserted shade."

The latter is obviously wrong (Gray was incapable of such metre), and the former is probably wrong also.

‡ Here also we follow Mason; the *North American Review* reads "our *labours* done."

in this part of the poem, but also completes the account of his whole day ; whereas, this evening scene being omitted, we have only his morning walk, and his noontide repose."

The first line of the 27th stanza reads,

"With gestures quaint, now smiling as in scorn."

After the 29th stanza, and before the Epitaph, the MS. contains the following omitted stanza :

"There scatter'd oft, the earliest of the year,
    By hands unseen are frequent violets found ;
The robin loves to build and warble there,
    And little footsteps lightly print the ground."

This—with two or three verbal changes only*—was inserted in all the editions up to 1753, when it was dropped. The omission was not made from any objection to the stanza in itself, but simply because it was too long a parenthesis in this place ; on the principle which he states in a letter to Dr. Beattie : "As to description, I have always thought that it made the most graceful ornament of poetry, but never ought to make the subject." The part was sacrificed for the good of the whole. Mason very justly remarked that "the lines, however, are in themselves exquisitely fine, and demand preservation."

The first line of the 31st stanza has "and his *heart* sincere."

The 32d and last stanza is as follows :

"No farther seek his merits to disclose,
    Nor seek to draw them from their dread abode—
(His frailties there in trembling hope repose);
    The bosom of his Father and his God."†

The Pembroke MS. has the following variations from the present version :

In the 1st stanza, "wind" for "winds."

2d stanza, "*Or* drowsy," etc.

5th stanza, "*and* the ecchoing horn."

6th stanza, "*Nor* climb his knees."

9th stanza, "*Awaits* alike." Probably this is also the reading of the Wrightson MS. Mitford gives it as noted by Mason, and it is retained by Gray in the ed. of 1768.

The 10th stanza begins,

"*Forgive*, ye Proud, *th' involuntary* fault
    If Memory *to these*," etc.,

the present readings ("Nor you," "impute to these," and "Mem'ry o'er their tomb") being inserted in the margin.

---

* See next page. The writer in the *North American Review* is our only authority for the stanza as given above. He appears to have had the photographic reproduction of the Wrightson MS., but we cannot vouch for the accuracy of his transcripts from it.

† The above are all the variations from the present text in the Wrightson MS. which are noted by the authorities on whom we have depended ; but we suspect that the following readings, mentioned by Mitford as in the MS., belong to *that* MS., as they are *not* found in the other : in the 7th stanza, "sickles" for "sickle ;" in 18th, "shrines" for "shrine." Two others (in stanzas 9th and 27th) are referred to in our account of the Pembroke MS. below.

F

The 12th stanza has "*reins* of empire," with "rod" in the margin.

In the 15th stanza, the word "lands" has been crossed out, and "fields" written above it.

The 17th has "*Or* shut the gates," etc.

In the 21st we have "fame and *epitaph* supply."

The 23d has "*And* in our ashes *glow*," the readings "Ev'n" and "live" being inserted in the margin.

The 27th stanza has "*would he* rove." We suspect that this is also the reading of the Wrightson MS., as Mitford says it is noted by Mason.

In the 28th stanza, the first line reads "*from* the custom'd hill."

In the 29th a word which we cannot make out has been erased, and "aged" substituted.

Before the Epitaph, two asterisks refer to the bottom of the page, where the following stanza is given, with the marginal note, "Omitted in 1753:"

> "There scatter'd oft, the earliest of the Year,
>   By Hands unseen, are Show'rs of Violets found;
> The Red-breast loves to build, and warble there,
>   And little Footsteps lightly print the Ground."

The last two lines of the 31st stanza (see note below) are pointed as follows :

> " He gave to Mis'ry all he had, a Tear,
>   He gain'd from Heav'n ('twas all he wish'd) a Friend."

Some of the peculiarities of spelling in this MS. are the following : "Curfeu ;" "Plowman ;" "Tinkleings ;" "mopeing ;" "ecchoing ;" "Huswife ;" " Ile " (aisle) ; "wast " (waste) ; "village-Hambden ;" "Rhimes ;" "spell't ;" "chearful ;" "born " (borne) ; etc.

Mitford, in his Life of Gray prefixed to the "Eton" edition of his Poems (edited by Rev. John Moultrie, 1847), says : " I possess many curious variations from the printed text, taken from a copy of it in his own handwriting." He adds specimens of these variations, a few of which differ from both the Wrightson and Pembroke MSS. We give these in our notes below. See on 12, 24, and 93.

Several localities have contended for the honor of being the scene of the *Elegy*, but the general sentiment has always, and justly, been in favor of Stoke-Pogis. It was there that Gray began the poem in 1742 ; and there, as we have seen, he finished it in 1750. In that churchyard his mother was buried, and there, at his request, his own remains were afterwards laid beside her. The scene is, moreover, in all respects in perfect keeping with the spirit of the poem.

According to the common Cambridge tradition, Granchester, a parish about two miles southwest of the University, to which Gray was in the habit of taking his "constitutional" daily, is the locality of the poem ; and the great bell of St. Mary's is the "curfew" of the first stanza. Another tradition makes a similar claim for Madingley, some three miles and a half northwest of Cambridge. Both places have churchyards such as the *Elegy* describes ; and this is about all that can be said in favor of their pretensions. There is also a parish called Burnham Beeches, in Buckinghamshire, which one writer at least has suggested as the scene of the poem, but for no better reason than that Gray once wrote a description of the place to Walpole, and casually mentioned the existence of certain "beeches," at the foot of which he would "squat," and "there grow to the trunk a whole morning." Gray's uncle had a seat in the neighborhood, and the poet often visited here, but the spot was not hallowed to him by the fond and tender associations that gathered about Stoke.

1. *The curfew.* Hales remarks: "It is a great mistake to suppose that the ringing of the curfew was, at its institution, a mark of Norman oppression. If such a custom was unknown before the Conquest, it only shows that the old English police was less well-regulated than that of many parts of the Continent, and how much the superior civilization of the Norman-French was needed. Fires were the curse of the timber-built towns of the Middle Ages: 'Solae pestes Londoniae sunt stultorum immodica potatio et *frequens incendium*' (Fitzstephen). The enforced extinction of domestic lights at an appointed signal was designed to be a safeguard against them."

Warton wanted to have this line read

"The curfew tolls!—the knell of parting day."

It is sufficient to say that Gray, as the manuscript shows, did not want it to read so, and that we much prefer his way to Warton's.

Mitford says that *toll* is "not the appropriate verb," as the curfew was rung, not tolled. We presume that depended, to some extent, on the fancy of the ringer. Milton (*Il Pens.* 76) speaks of the curfew as

"Swinging slow with sullen roar."

Gray himself quotes here Dante, *Purgat.* 8 :

—"squilla di lontano
Che paia 'l giorno pianger, che si muore ;"

and we cannot refrain from adding, for the benefit of those unfamiliar with Italian, Longfellow's exquisite translation :

—"from far away a bell
That seemeth to deplore the dying day."

Mitford quotes (incorrectly, as often) Dryden, *Prol. to Troilus and Cressida*, 22 :

"That tolls the knell for their departed sense."

On *parting*=departing, cf. Shakes. *Cor.* v. 6 : "When I parted hence ;" Goldsmith, *D. V.* 171 : "Beside the bed where parting life was laid," etc.

2. *The lowing herd wind*, etc. *Wind*, and not *winds*, is the reading of the MS. (see fac-simile of this stanza on p. 73) and of *all* the early editions—that of 1768, Mason's, Wakefield's, Mathias's, etc.—but we find no note of the fact in Mitford's or any other of the more recent editions, which have substituted *winds*. Whether the change was made as an amendment or accidentally, we do not know ;* but the original reading

* Very likely the latter, as we have seen that *winds* appears in the unauthorized version of the *London Magazine* (March, 1751), where it may be a misprint, like the others noted above.

seems to us by far the better one. The poet does not refer to the herd as an aggregate, but to the animals that compose it. He sees, not *it*, but "*them* on their winding way." The ordinary reading mars both the meaning and the melody of the line.

3. The critic of the *N. A. Review* points out that this line "is quite peculiar in its possible transformations. We have made," he adds, "twenty different versions preserving the rhythm, the general sentiment, and the rhyming word. Any one of these variations might be, not inappropriately, substituted for the original reading."

Luke quotes Spenser, *F. Q.* vi. 7, 39: "And now she was uppon the weary way."

6. *Air* is of course the object, not the subject of the verb.

7. *Save where the beetle*, etc. Cf. Collins, *Ode to Evening:*

> "Now air is hush'd, save where the weak-eyed bat
> With short shrill shriek flits by on leathern wing,
>   Or where the beetle winds
>   His small but sullen horn,
> As oft he rises 'midst the twilight path,
> Against the pilgrim borne in heedless hum."

and *Macbeth*, iii. 2:

> "Ere the bat hath flown
> His cloister'd flight; ere to black Hecate's summons
> The shard-borne beetle, with his drowsy hums,
> Hath rung night's yawning peal," etc.

10. *The moping owl.* Mitford quotes Ovid, *Met.* v. 550: "Ignavus bubo, dirum mortalibus omen;" Thomson, *Winter*, 114:

> "Assiduous in his bower the wailing owl
> Plies his sad song;"

and Mallet, *Excursion:*

> "the wailing owl
> Screams solitary to the mournful moon."

12. *Her ancient solitary reign.* Cf. Virgil, *Geo.* iii. 476: "desertaque regna pastorum." A MS. variation of this line mentioned by Mitford is, "Molest and pry into her ancient reign."

13. "As he stands in the churchyard, he thinks only of the poorer people, because the better-to-do lay interred inside the church. Tennyson (*In Mem.* x.) speaks of resting

---

We may remark here that the edition of 1768—the *editio princeps* of the *collected* Poems—was issued under Gray's own supervision, and is printed with remarkable accuracy. We have detected only one indubitable error of the type in the entire volume. Certain peculiarities of spelling were probably intentional, as we find the like in the facsimiles of the poet's manuscripts. The many quotations from Greek, Latin, and Italian are correctly given (according to the received texts of the time), and the references to authorities, so far as we have verified them, are equally exact. The book throughout bears the marks of Gray's scholarly and critical habits, and we may be sure that the poems appear in precisely the form which he meant they should retain. In doubtful cases, therefore, we have generally followed this edition. Mason's (the *second* edition: York, 1778) is also carefully edited and printed, and its readings seldom vary from Gray's. All of Mitford's that we have examined swarm with errors, especially in the notes. Pickering's (1835), edited by Mitford, is perhaps the worst of all. The Boston ed. (Little, Brown, & Co., 1853) is a pretty careful reproduction of Pickering's, with all its inaccuracies.

'beneath the clover sod
That takes the sunshine and the rains,
Or where the kneeling hamlet drains
The chalice of the grapes of God.'

In Gray's time, and long before, and some time after it, the former resting-place was for the poor, the latter for the rich. It was so in the first instance, for two reasons : (i.) the interior of the church was regarded as of great sanctity, and all who could sought a place in it, the most dearly coveted spot being near the high altar ; (ii.) when elaborate tombs were the fashion, they were built inside the church for the sake of security, 'gay tombs' being liable to be 'robb'd' (see the funeral dirge in Webster's *White Devil*). As these two considerations gradually ceased to have power, and other considerations of an opposite tendency began to prevail, the inside of the church became comparatively deserted, except when ancestral reasons gave no choice" (Hales).

17. Cf. Milton, *Arcades*, 56 : "the odorous breath of morn ;" *P. L.* ix. 192 :

" Now when as sacred light began to dawn
In Eden on the humid flowers that breath'd
Their morning incense," etc.

18. Hesiod (Epy. 568) calls the swallow ὀρθογόη χελιδών. Cf. Virgil, *Æn.* viii. 455 :

" Evandrum ex humili tecto lux suscitat alma,
Et matutini volucrum sub culmine cantus."

19. *The cock's shrill clarion.* Cf. Philips, *Cyder*, i. 753 :

"When chanticleer with clarion shrill recalls
The tardy day ;"

Milton, *P. L.* vii. 443 :

"The crested cock, whose clarion sounds
The silent hours ;"

Hamlet, i. 1 :

" The cock that is the trumpet to the morn ;"

Quarles, *Argalus and Parthenia :*

" I slept not till the early bugle-horn
Of chaunticlere had summon'd in the morn ;"

and Thomas Kyd, *England's Parnassus :*

"The cheerful cock, the sad night's trumpeter,
Wayting upon the rising of the sunne ;
The wandering swallow with her broken song," etc.

20. *Their lowly bed.* Wakefield remarks : " Some readers, keeping in mind the 'narrow cell' above, have mistaken the 'lowly bed' in this verse for the grave—a most puerile and ridiculous blunder ;" and Mitford says : " Here the epithet 'lowly,' as applied to 'bed,' occasions some ambiguity as to whether the poet meant the bed on which they sleep, or the grave in which they are laid, which in poetry is called a 'lowly bed.' Of course the former is designed ; but Mr. Lloyd, in his Latin translation, mistook it for the latter."

21. Cf. Lucretius, iii. 894:

> "Jam jam non domus accipiet te laeta, neque uxor
> Optima nec dulces occurrent oscula nati
> Praeripere et tacita pectus dulcedine tangent;"

and Horace, *Epod.* ii. 39:

> "Quod si pudica mulier in partem juvet
> Domum atque dulces liberos
> * * * * * * *
> Sacrum vetustis exstruat lignis focum
> Lassi sub adventum viri," etc.

Mitford quotes Thomson, *Winter*, 311:

> "In vain for him the officious wife prepares
> The fire fair-blazing, and the vestment warm;
> In vain his little children, peeping out
> Into the mingling storm, demand their sire
> With tears of artless innocence."

Wakefield cites *The Idler*, 103: "There are few things, not purely evil, of which we can say without some emotion of uneasiness, *this is the last.*"

22. *Ply her evening care.* Mitford says, "To *ply a care* is an expression that is not proper to our language, and was probably formed for the rhyme *share.*" Hales remarks: "This is probably the kind of phrase which led Wordsworth to pronounce the language of the *Elegy* unintelligible. Compare his own

> 'And she I cherished *turned her wheel*
> Beside an English fire.' "

23. *No children run*, etc. Hales quotes Burns, *Cotter's Saturday Night*, 21:

> "Th' expectant wee-things, toddlin, stacher through
> To meet their Dad, wi' flichterin noise an' glee."

24. Among Mitford's MS. variations we find "coming kiss." Wakefield compares Virgil, *Geo.* ii. 523:

> "Interea dulces pendent circum oscula nati;"

and Mitford adds from Dryden,

> "Whose little arms about thy legs are cast,
> And climbing for a kiss prevent their mother's haste."

Cf. Thomson, *Liberty*, iii. 171:

> "His little children climbing for a kiss."

26. *The stubborn glebe.* Cf. Gay, *Fables*, ii. 15:

> "'Tis mine to tame the stubborn glebe."

Broke = broken, as often in poetry, especially in the Elizabethan writers. See Abbott, *Shakes. Gr.* 343.

27. *Drive their team afield.* Cf. *Lycidas*, 27: "We drove afield;" and Dryden, *Virgil's Ecl.* ii. 38: "With me to drive afield."

28. *Their sturdy stroke.* Cf. Spenser, *Shep. Kal.* Feb.:

> "But to the roote bent his sturdy stroake,
> And made many wounds in the wast [wasted] Oake;"

and Dryden, *Geo.* iii. 639 :

> "Labour him with many a sturdy stroke."

30. As Mitford remarks, *obscure* and *poor* make "a very imperfect rhyme ;" and the same might be said of *toil* and *smile*.

33. Mitford suggests that Gray had in mind these verses from his friend West's *Monody on Queen Caroline :*

> "Ah, me ! what boots us all our boasted power,
>   Our golden treasure, and our purple state ;
>   They cannot ward the inevitable hour,
>   Nor stay the fearful violence of fate."

Hurd compares Cowley :

> "Beauty, and strength, and wit, and wealth, and power,
>   Have their short flourishing hour ;
>   And love to see themselves, and smile,
>   And joy in their pre-eminence a while :
>   Even so in the same land
>   Poor weeds, rich corn, gay flowers together stand ;
>   Alas ! Death mows down all with an impartial hand."

35. The edition of 1768, like the **Pembroke** (and probably the other) MS., has "Awaits," but we have decided to retain the modern "Await."

36. Hayley, in the Life of Crashaw, *Biographia Britannica*, says that this line is "literally translated from the Latin prose of Bartholinus in his Danish Antiquities."

39. *Fretted.* The *fret* is, strictly, an ornament used in classical architecture, formed by small fillets intersecting each other at right angles. Parker (*Glossary of Architecture*) derives the word from the Latin *fretum*, a strait ; and Hales from *ferrum*, iron, through the Italian *ferrata*, an iron grating. It is more likely (see Stratmann and Wb.) from the A. S. *frætu*, an ornament.

Cf. *Hamlet*, ii. 2 :

> "This majestical roof fretted with golden fire ;"

and *Cymbeline*, ii. 4 :

> "The roof o' the chamber
>   With golden cherubins is fretted."

40. *The pealing anthem.* Cf. *Il Penseroso*, 161 :

> "There let the pealing organ blow
>   To the full-voiced quire below,
>   In service high, and anthem clear," etc.

41. *Storied urn.* Cf. *Il Pens.* 159 : "storied windows richly dight." On *animated bust*, cf. Pope, *Temple of Fame*, 73 : "Heroes in animated marble frown ;" and Virgil, *Æn.* vi. 847 : "spirantia aera."

43. *Provoke.* Mitford considers this use of the word "unusually bold, to say the least." It is simply the etymological meaning, *to call forth* (Latin, *provocare*). See Wb. Cf. Pope, *Ode :*

> "But when our country's cause provokes to arms."

44. *Dull cold ear.* Cf. Shakes. *Hen. VIII.* iii. 2 : "And sleep in dull, cold marble."

46. *Pregnant with celestial fire.* This phrase has been copied by Cowper in his *Boadicea,* which is said (see notes of "Globe" ed.) to have been written after reading Hume's History, in 1780:

> "Such the bard's prophetic words,
> Pregnant with celestial fire,
> Bending as he swept the chords
> Of his sweet but awful lyre."

47. Mitford quotes Ovid, *Ep.* v. 86 :

> "Sunt mihi quas possint sceptra decere manus."

48. *Living lyre.* Cf. Cowley :

> "Begin the song, and strike the living lyre;"

and Pope, *Windsor Forest,* 281 :

> "Who now shall charm the shades where Cowley strung
> His living harp, and lofty Denham sung?"

50. Cf. Browne, *Religio Medici :* "Rich with the spoils of nature."

51. "*Rage* is often used in the post-Elizabethan writers of the 17th century, and in the 18th century writers, for inspiration, enthusiasm" (Hales). Cf. Cowley :

> "Who brought green poesy to her perfect age,
> And made that art which was a rage?"

and Tickell, *Prol. :*

> "How hard the task ! How rare the godlike rage !"

Cf. also the use of the Latin *rabies* for the "divine afflatus," as in *Æneid,* vi. 49.

53. *Full many a gem,* etc. Cf. Bishop Hall, *Contemplations :* "There is many a rich stone laid up in the bowells of the earth, many a fair pearle in the bosome of the sea, that never was seene, nor never shall bee."

Purest ray serene. As Hales remarks, this is a favourite arrangement of epithets with Milton. Cf. *Hymn on Nativity :* "flower-inwoven tresses torn ;" *Comus :* "beckoning shadows dire ;" "every alley green," etc. ; *L'Allegro :* "native wood-notes wild ;" *Lycidas :* "sad occasion dear ;" "blest kingdoms meek," etc.

55. *Full many a flower,* etc. Cf. Pope, *Rape of the Lock,* iv. 158 :

> "Like roses that in deserts bloom and die."

Mitford cites Chamberlayne, *Pharonida,* ii. 4 :

> "Like beauteous flowers which vainly waste their scent
> Of odours in unhaunted deserts ;"

and Young, *Univ. Pass.* sat. v. :

> "In distant wilds, by human eyes unseen,
> She rears her flowers, and spreads her velvet green ;
> Pure gurgling rills the lonely desert trace,
> And waste their music on the savage race ;"

and Philip, *Thule :*

> "Like woodland flowers, which paint the desert glades,
> And waste their sweets in unfrequented shades."

Hales quotes Waller's

> "Go, lovely rose,
> Tell her that's young
> And shuns to have her graces spied,
> That hadst thou sprung
> In deserts where no men abide
> Thou must have uncommended died."

On *desert air*, cf. *Macbeth*, iv. 3 : "That would be howl'd out in the desert air."

57. It was in 1636 that John Hampden, of Buckinghamshire (a cousin of Oliver Cromwell), refused to pay the ship-money tax which Charles I. was levying without the authority of Parliament.

58. *Little tyrant.* Cf. Thomson, *Winter* :

> "With open freedom little tyrants raged."

The artists who have illustrated this passage (see, for instance, *Favourite English Poems*, p. 305, and *Harper's Monthly*, vol. vii. p. 3) appear to understand "little" as equivalent to *juvenile.* If that had been the meaning, the poet would have used some other phrase than "of his fields," or "his lands," as he first wrote it.

59. *Some mute inglorious Milton.* Cf. Phillips, preface to *Theatrum Poetarum :* "Even the very names of some who having perhaps been comparable to Homer for heroic poesy, or to Euripides for tragedy, yet nevertheless sleep inglorious in the crowd of the forgotten vulgar."

60. *Some Cromwell*, etc. Hales remarks : "The prejudice against Cromwell was extremely strong throughout the 18th century, even amongst the more liberal-minded. That cloud of 'detractions rude,' of which Milton speaks in his noble sonnet to our 'chief of men' as in his own day enveloping the great republican leader, still lay thick and heavy over him. His wise statesmanship, his unceasing earnestness, his high-minded purpose, were not yet seen."

After this stanza Thomas Edwards, the author of the *Canons of Criticism*, would add the following, to supply what he deemed a defect in the poem :

> "Some lovely fair, whose unaffected charms
> Shone with attraction to herself alone ;
> Whose beauty might have bless'd a monarch's arms,
> Whose virtue cast a lustre on a throne.

> "That humble beauty warm'd an honest heart,
> And cheer'd the labours of a faithful spouse ;
> That virtue form'd for every decent part
> The healthful offspring that adorn'd their house."

Edwards was an able critic, but it is evident that he was no poet.

63. Mitford quotes Tickell :

> "To scatter blessings o'er the British land ;"

and Mrs. Behn :

> "Is scattering plenty over all the land."

66. *Their growing virtues.* That is, the growth of their virtues.

67. *To wade through slaughter,* etc.   Cf. Pope, *Temp. of Fame,* 347 :
> "And swam to empire through the purple flood."

68. Cf. Shakes. *Hen. V.* iii. 3 :
> "The gates of mercy shall be all shut up."

70. *To quench the blushes,* etc.   Cf. Shakes. *W. T.* iv. 3 :
> "Come, quench your blushes, and present yourself."

73. *Far from the madding crowd's,* etc.   Rogers quotes Drummond :
> "Far from the madding worldling's hoarse discords."

Mitford points out "the ambiguity of this couplet, which indeed gives a sense exactly contrary to that intended ; to avoid which one must break the grammatical construction." The poet's meaning is, however, clear enough.

75. Wakefield quotes Pope, *Epitaph on Fenton :*
> "Foe to loud praise, and friend to learned ease,
> Content with science in the vale of peace."

77. *These bones.* "The bones of these. So *is* is often used in Latin, especially by Livy, as in v. 22 : '*Ea* sola pecunia,' the money derived from that sale, etc." (Hales).

84. *That teach.* Mitford censures *teach* as ungrammatical ; but it may be justified as a "construction according to sense."

85. Hales remarks : "At the first glance it might seem that *to dumb Forgetfulness a prey* was in apposition to *who,* and the meaning was, 'Who that now lies forgotten,' etc. ; in which case the second line of the stanza must be closely connected with the fourth ; for the question of the passage is not 'Who ever died ?' but 'Who ever died without wishing to be remembered ?' But in this way of interpreting this difficult stanza (i.) there is comparatively little force in the appositional phrase, and (ii.) there is a certain awkwardness in deferring so long the clause (virtually adverbial though apparently coördinate) in which, as has just been noticed, the point of the question really lies. Perhaps therefore it is better to take the phrase *to dumb Forgetfulness a prey* as in fact the completion of the predicate *resign'd,* and interpret thus : Who ever resigned this life of his with all its pleasures and all its pains to be utterly ignored and forgotten? = who ever, when resigning it, reconciled himself to its being forgotten? In this case the second half of the stanza echoes the thought of the first half."

We give the note in full, and leave the reader to take his choice of the two interpretations. For ourself, we incline to the first rather than the second. We prefer to take *to dumb Forgetfulness a prey* as appositional and proleptic, and not as the grammatical complement of *resigned :* Who, yielding himself up a prey to dumb Forgetfulness, ever resigned this life without casting a longing, lingering look behind ?

90. *Pious* is used in the sense of the Latin *pius.* Ovid has "piae lacrimae." Mitford quotes Pope, *Elegy on an Unfortunate Lady,* 49 :
> "No friend's complaint, no kind domestic tear
> Pleas'd thy pale ghost, or grac'd thy mournful bier ;
> By foreign hands thy dying eyes were clos'd."

"In this stanza," says Hales, "he answers in an exquisite manner the two questions, or rather the one question twice repeated, of the preceding stanza. . . . What he would say is that every one while a spark of life yet remains in him yearns for some kindly loving remembrance ; nay, even after the spark is quenched, even when all is dust and ashes, that yearning must still be felt."

91, 92. Mitford paraphrases the couplet thus: "The voice of Nature still cries from the tomb in the language of the epitaph inscribed upon it, which still endeavours to connect us with the living ; the fires of former affection are still alive beneath our ashes."

Cf. Chaucer, *C. T.* 3880 :

> "Yet in our ashen cold is fire yreken."

Gray himself quotes Petrarch, *Sonnet* 169 :

> "Ch'i veggio nel pensier, dolce mio fuoco,
> Fredda una lingua e due begli occhi chiusi,
> Rimaner doppo noi pien di faville,"

translated by Nott as follows :

> "These, my sweet fair, so warns prophetic thought,
> Clos'd thy bright eye, and mute thy poet's tongue,
> E'en after death shall still with sparks be fraught,"

the "these" meaning his love and his songs concerning it. Gray translated this sonnet into Latin elegiacs, the last line being rendered,

> "Ardebitque urna multa favilla mea."

93. On a MS. variation of this stanza given by Mitford, see p. 80, footnote.

95. *Chance* is virtually an adverb here = perchance.

98. *The peep of dawn.* Mitford quotes *Comus*, 138 :

> "Ere the blabbing eastern scout,
> The nice morn, on the Indian steep
> From her cabin'd loop-hole peep."

99. Cf. Milton, *P. L.* v. 428 :

> "though from off the boughs each morn
> We brush mellifluous dews;"

and *Arcades*, 50 :

> "And from the boughs brush off the evil dew."

Wakefield quotes Thomson, *Spring*, 103 :

> "Oft let me wander o'er the dewy fields,
> Where freshness breathes, and dash the trembling drops
> From the bent brush, as through the verdant maze
> Of sweetbrier hedges I pursue my walk."

100. *Upland lawn.* Cf. Milton, *Lycidas*, 25 :

> "Ere the high lawns appear'd
> Under the opening eyelids of the morn."

In *L'Allegro*, 92, we have "upland hamlets," where Hales thinks "upland = country, as opposed to town." He adds, "Gray in his *Elegy* seems to use the word loosely for 'on the higher ground;' perhaps he took it from Milton, without quite understanding in what sense Milton uses it." We doubt whether Hales understands Milton here. It is true that *upland* used to mean country, as *uplanders* meant countrymen, and *uplandish* countrified (see Nares and Wb.), but the other meaning is older than Milton (see Halliwell's *Dict. of Archaic Words*), and Johnson, Keightley, and others are probably right in considering "upland hamlets" an instance of it. Masson, in his recent edition of Milton (1875), explains the "upland hamlets" as "little villages among the slopes, away from the river-meadows and the hay-making."

101. As Mitford remarks, *beech* and *stretch* form an imperfect rhyme.

102. Luke quotes Spenser, *Ruines of Rome*, st. 28:

> "Shewing her wreathed rootes and naked armes."

103. *His listless length.* Hales compares *King Lear*, i. 4: "If you will measure your lubber's length again, tarry." Cf. also *Brittain's Ida* (formerly ascribed to Spenser, but rejected by the best editors), iii. 2:

> "Her goodly length stretcht on a lilly-bed."

104. Cf. Thomson, *Spring*, 644: "divided by a babbling brook;" and Horace, *Od.* iii. 13, 15:

> "unde loquaces
> Lymphae desiliunt tuae."

Wakefield quotes *As You Like It*, ii. 1:

> "As he lay along
> Under an oak whose antique root peeps out
> Upon the brook that brawls along this road."

105. *Smiling as in scorn.* Cf. Shakes. *Pass. Pilgrim*, 14:

> "Yet at my parting sweetly did she smile,
> In scorn or friendship, nill I construe whether."

and Skelton, *Prol. to B. of C.*:

> "Smylynge half in scorne
> At our foly."

107. *Woeful-wan.* Mitford says: "*Woeful-wan* is not a legitimate compound, and must be divided into two separate words, for such they are, when released from the *handcuffs* of the hyphen." The hyphen is not in the edition of 1768, and we should omit it if it were not found in the Pembroke MS.

Wakefield quotes Spenser, *Shep. Kal.* Jan.:

> "For pale and wanne he was (alas the while!)
> May seeme he lovd, or els some care he tooke."

108. "*Hopeless* is here used in a proleptic or anticipatory way" (Hales).

109. *Custom'd* is Gray's word, not *'custom'd*, as usually printed. See either Wb. or Worc. s. v. Cf. Milton, *Ep. Damonis:* "Simul assueta seditque sub ulmo."

114. *Churchway path.* Cf. Shakes. *M. N. D.* v. 2:

> "Now it is the time of night,
>   That the graves all gaping wide,
> Every one lets forth his sprite
>   In the churchway paths to glide."

115. *For thou canst read.* The "hoary-headed swain" of course could *not* read.

116. *Grav'd.* The old form of the participle is *graven*, but *graved* is also in good use. The old preterite *grove* is obsolete.

117. *The lap of earth.* Cf. Spenser, *F. Q.* v. 7, 9 :

> "For other beds the Priests there used none,
>   But on their mother Earths deare lap did lie;"

and Milton, *P. L.* x. 777 :

> "How glad would lay me down,
>   As in my mother's lap!"

Lucretius (i. 291) has "gremium matris terrai." Mitford adds the pathetic sentence of Pliny, *Hist. Nat.* ii. 63 : "Nam terra novissime complexa gremio jam a reliqua natura abnegatos, tum maxime, ut mater, operit."

123. *He gave to misery all he had, a tear.* This is the pointing of the line in the MSS. and in all the early editions except that of Mathias, who seems to be responsible for the change (adopted by the recent editors, almost without exception) to,

> "He gave to Misery (all he had) a tear."

This alters the meaning, mars the rhythm, and spoils the sentiment. If one does not see the difference at once, it would be useless to try to make him see it. Mitford, who ought to have known better, not only thrusts in the parenthesis, but quotes this from Pope's Homer as an illustration of it :

> "His fame ('tis all the dead can have) shall live."

126. Mitford says that *Or* in this line should be *Nor.* Yes, if "draw" is an imperative, like "seek ;" no, if it is an infinitive, in the same construction as "to disclose." That the latter was the construction the poet had in mind is evident from the form of the stanza in the Wrightson MS., where "seek" is repeated :

> "No farther seek his merits to disclose,
>   Nor seek to draw them from their dread abode."

127. *In trembling hope.* Gray quotes Petrarch, *Sonnet* 104 : " paventosa speme." Cf. Lucan, *Pharsalia*, vii. 297 : " Spe trepido ;" Mallet, *Funeral Hymn*, 473 :

> "With trembling tenderness of hope and fear;"

and Beaumont, *Psyche*, xv. 314 :

> "Divided here twixt trembling hope and fear."

Hooker (*Eccl. Pol.* i.) defines hope as " a trembling expectation of things far removed."

ODE ON THE SPRING.

THE original manuscript title of this ode was "Noontide." It was first printed in Dodsley's *Collection*, vol. ii. p. 271, under the title of "Ode."

1. *The rosy-bosom'd Hours.* Cf. Milton, *Comus*, 984: "The Graces and the rosy-bosom'd Hours;" and Thomson, *Spring*, 1007:

"The rosy-bosom'd Spring
To weeping Fancy pines."

The *Horæ*, or hours, according to the Homeric idea, were the goddesses of the seasons, the course of which was symbolically represented by "the dance of the Hours." They were often described, in connection with the Graces, Hebe, and Aphrodite, as accompanying with their dancing the songs of the Muses and the lyre of Apollo. Long after the time of Homer they continued to be regarded as the givers of the seasons, especially spring and autumn, or "Nature in her bloom and her maturity." At first there were only two Horæ, Thallo (or Spring) and Karpo (or Autumn); but later the number was three, like that of the Graces. In art they are represented as blooming maidens, bearing the products of the seasons.

2. *Fair Venus' train.* The Hours adorned Aphrodite (Venus) as she rose from the sea, and are often associated with her by Homer, Hesiod, and other classical writers. Wakefield remarks: "Venus is here employed, in conformity to the mythology of the Greeks, as the source of creation and beauty."

3. *Long-expecting.* Waiting long for the spring. Sometimes incorrectly printed "long-expected." Cf. Dryden, *Astræa Redux*, 132: "To flowers that in its womb expecting lie."

4. *The purple year.* Cf. the *Pervigilium Veneris*, 13: "Ipsa gemmis purpurantem pingit annum floribus;" Pope, *Pastorals*, i. 28: "And lavish Nature paints the purple year;" and Mallet, *Zephyr:* "Gales that wake the purple year."

5. *The Attic warbler.* The nightingale, called "the Attic bird," either because it was so common in Attica, or from the old legend that Philomela (or, as some say, Procne), the daughter of a king of Attica, was changed into a nightingale. Cf. Milton's description of Athens (*P. R.* iv. 245):

> "where the Attic bird
> Trills her thick-warbled notes the summer long."

Cf. Ovid, *Hal.* 110: "Attica avis verna sub tempestate queratus;" and Propertius, ii. 16, 6: "Attica volucris."

Pours her throat is a metonymy. H. p. 85. Cf. Pope, *Essay on Man*, iii. 33: "Is it for thee the linnet pours her throat?"

6, 7. Cf. Thomson, *Spring*, 577:

> "From the first note the hollow cuckoo sings,
> The symphony of spring."

9, 10. Cf. Milton, *Comus*, 989:

> "And west winds with musky wing
> About the cedarn alleys fling
> Nard and cassia's balmy smells."

12. Cf. Milton, *P. L.* iv. 245: "Where the unpierc'd shade Imbrown'd the noontide bowers;" Pope, *Eloisa*, 170: "And breathes a browner horror on the woods;" Thomson, *Castle of Indolence*, i. 38: "Or Autumn's varied shades imbrown the walls."

According to Ruskin (*Modern Painters*, vol. iii. p. 241, Amer. ed.) there is no brown in nature. After remarking that Dante "does not acknowledge the existence of the colour of *brown* at all," he goes on to say: "But one day, just when I was puzzling myself about this, I happened to be sitting by one of our best living modern colourists, watching him at his work, when he said, suddenly and by mere accident, after we had been talking about other things, 'Do you know I have found that there is no *brown* in nature? What we call brown is always a variety either of orange or purple. It never can be represented by umber, unless altered by contrast.' It is curious how far the significance of this remark extends, how exquisitely it illustrates and confirms the mediæval sense of hue," etc.

13. *O'ercanopies the glade.* Gray himself quotes Shakes. *M. N. D.* ii. 1 : "A bank o'ercanopied with luscious woodbine." * Cf. Fletcher, *Purple Island,* i. 5, 30 : " The beech shall yield a cool, safe canopy ;" and Milton, *Comus,* 543 : " a bank, With ivy canopied."

15. *Rushy brink.* Cf. *Comus,* 890 : " By the rushy-fringed bank."

19, 20. These lines, as first printed, read :

> " How low, how indigent the proud!
> How little are the great !"

22. *The panting herds.* Cf. Pope, *Past.* ii. 87 : " To closer shades the panting flocks remove."

23. *The peopled air.* Cf. Walton, *C. A. :* " Now the wing'd people of the sky shall sing ;" Beaumont, *Psyche :* " Every tree empeopled was with birds of softest throats."

24. *The busy murmur.* Cf. Milton, *P. R.* iv. 248 : " bees' industrious murmur."

25. *The insect youth.* Perhaps suggested by a line in Green's *Hermitage,* quoted in a letter of Gray to Walpole : " From maggot-youth through change of state," etc. See on 31 below.

26. *The honied spring.* Cf. Milton, *Il Pens.* 142 : " the bee with honied thigh ;" and *Lyc.* 140 : " the honied showers."

" There has of late arisen," says Johnson in his Life of Gray, " a practice of giving to adjectives derived from substantives the termination of participles, such as the *cultured plain,* the *daisied bank ;* but I am sorry to see in the lines of a scholar like Gray the *honied* spring." But, as we have seen, *honied* is found in Milton ; and Shakespeare also uses it in *Hen. V.* i. 1 : " honey'd sentences." *Mellitus* is used by Cicero, Horace, and Catullus. The editor of an English dictionary, as Lord Grenville has remarked, ought to know "that the ready conversion of our substances into verbs, participles, and participial adjectives is of the very essence of our tongue, derived from its Saxon origin, and a main source of its energy and richness."

27. *The liquid noon.* Gray quotes Virgil, *Geo.* iv. 59 : " Nare per aestatem liquidam."

30. *Quick-glancing to the sun.* Gray quotes Milton, *P. L.* vii. 405 :

> " Sporting with quick glance,
> Show to the sun their waved coats dropt with gold."

31. Gray here quotes Green, *Grotto :* " While insects from the threshold

---

* The reading of the folio of 1623 is :

> " I know a banke where the wilde time blowes,
> Where Oxslips and the nodding Violet growes,
> Quite ouer-cannoped with luscious woodbine."

Dyce and some other modern editors read,

> " Quite overcanopied with lush woodbine."

preach." In a letter to Walpole, he says : "I send you a bit of a thing for two reasons : first, because it is of one of your favourites, Mr. M. Green ; and next, because I would do justice. The thought on which my second Ode turns [this Ode, afterwards placed first by Gray] is manifestly stole from hence ; not that I knew it at the time, but having seen this many years before, to be sure it imprinted itself on my memory, and, forgetting the Author, I took it for my own." Then comes the quotation from Green's *Grotto*. The passage referring to the insects is as follows :

> "To the mind's ear, and inward sight,
> There silence speaks, and shade gives light :
> While insects from the threshold preach,
> And minds dispos'd to musing teach ;
> Proud of strong limbs and painted hues,
> They perish by the slightest bruise ;
> Or maladies begun within
> Destroy more slow life's frail machine :
> From maggot-youth, thro' change of state,
> They feel like us the turns of fate :
> Some born to creep have liv'd to fly,
> And chang'd earth's cells for dwellings high :
> And some that did their six wings keep,
> Before they died, been forc'd to creep.
> They politics, like ours, profess ;
> The greater prey upon the less.
> Some strain on foot huge loads to bring,
> Some toil incessant on the wing :
> Nor from their vigorous schemes desist
> Till death ; and then they are never mist.
> Some frolick, toil, marry, increase,
> Are sick and well, have war and peace ;
> And broke with age in half a day,
> Yield to successors, and away."

47. *Painted plumage.* Cf. Pope, *Windsor Forest*, 118 : " His painted wings ;" and Milton, *P. L.* vii. 433 :

> " From branch to branch the smaller birds with song
> Solaced the woods, and spread their painted wings."

See also Virgil, *Geo.* iii. 243, and *Æn.* iv. 525 : " pictaeque volucres ;" and Phædrus, *Fab.* iii. 18 : " pictisque plumis."

G

ODE ON THE DEATH OF A FAVOURITE CAT.

This ode first appeared in Dodsley's *Collection*, vol. ii. p. 274, with some variations noticed below. Walpole, after the death of Gray, placed the china vase on a pedestal at Strawberry Hill, with a few lines of the ode for an inscription.

In a letter to Walpole, dated March 1, 1747, Gray refers to the subject of the ode in the following jocose strain : "As one ought to be particularly careful to avoid blunders in a compliment of condolence, it would be a sensible satisfaction to me (before I testify my sorrow, and the sincere part I take in your misfortune) to know for certain who it is I lament. I knew Zara and Selima (Selima, was it? or Fatima?), or rather I knew them both together ; for I cannot justly say which was which. Then as to your handsome Cat, the name you distinguish her by, I am no less at a loss, as well knowing one's handsome cat is always the cat one likes best; or if one be alive and the other dead, it is usually the latter that is the handsomest. Besides, if the point were never so clear, I hope you do not think me so ill-bred or so imprudent as to forfeit all my interest in the survivor ; oh no! I would rather seem to mistake, and imagine to be sure it must be the tabby one that had met with this sad accident. Till this affair is a little better determined, you will excuse me if I do not begin to cry,

Tempus inane peto, requiem spatiumque doloris.

" . . . Heigh ho ! I feel (as you to be sure have done long since) that I have very little to say, at least in prose. Somebody will be the better for it ; I do not mean you, but your Cat, feuë Mademoiselle Selime, whom I am about to immortalize for one week or fortnight, as follows : [the Ode follows, which we need not reprint here].

"There's a poem for you, it is rather too long for an Epitaph."

2. Cf. Lady M. W. Montagu, *Town Eclogues :*

"Where the tall jar erects its stately pride,
With antic shapes in China's azure dyed."

3. *The azure flowers that blow.* Johnson and Wakefield find fault with this as redundant, but it is no more so than poetic usage allows. In the *Progress of Poesy*, i. 1, we have again : " The laughing flowers that round them blow." Cf. *Comus*, 992 :

"Iris there with humid bow
Waters the odorous banks that blow
Flowers of more mingled hue
Than her purfled scarf can shew."

4. *Tabby.* For the derivation of this word from the French *tabis*, a kind of silk, see Wb. In the first ed. the 5th line preceded the 4th.

6. *The lake.* In the mock-heroic vein that runs through the whole poem.

11. *Jet.* This word comes, through the French, from Gagai, a town in Lycia, where the mineral was first obtained.

14. *Two angel forms.* In the first ed. "two beauteous forms," which Mitford prefers to the present reading, "as the images of *angel* and *genii* interfere with each other, and bring different associations to the mind."

15. *Tyrian hue.* Explained by the "purple" in next line; an allusion to the famous Tyrian dye of the ancients. Cf. Pope, *Windsor Forest*, 142: "with fins of Tyrian dye."

17. Cf. Virgil, *Geo.* iv. 274:

> "*Aureus* ipse ; sed in foliis, quae plurima circum
> Funduntur, violae *sublucet purpura* nigrae."

See also Pope, *Windsor Forest*, 332: "His shining horns diffus'd a golden glow ;" *Temple of Fame*, 253: "And lucid amber casts a golden gleam."

24. In the 1st ed. "What cat's a foe to fish?" and in the next line, "with eyes intent."

31. *Eight times.* Alluding to the proverbial "nine lives" of the cat.

34. *No dolphin came.* An allusion to the story of Arion, who when thrown overboard by the sailors for the sake of his wealth was borne safely to land by a dolphin.

No Nereid stirr'd. Cf. Milton, *Lycidas*, 50:

> "Where were ye, Nymphs, when the remorseless deep
> Closed o'er the head of your lov'd Lycidas ?"

35, 36. The reading of 1st ed. is,

> "Nor cruel Tom nor Harry heard.
> What favourite has a friend ?"

40. The 1st ed. has "Not all that strikes," etc.

42. *Nor all that glisters gold.* A favourite proverb with the old English poets. Cf. Chaucer, *C. T.* 16430:

> "But all thing which that shineth as the gold
> Ne is no gold, as I have herd it told ;"

Spenser, *F. Q.* ii. 8, 14:

> "Yet gold all is not, that doth golden seeme ;"

Shakes. *M. of V.* ii. 7:

> "All that glisters is not gold ;
> Often have you heard that told ;"

Dryden, *Hind and Panther*:

> "All, as they say, that glitters is not gold."

Other examples might be given. *Glisten* is not found in Shakes. or Milton, but both use *glister* several times. See *W. T.* iii. 2 ; *Rich. II.* iii. 3 ; *T. A.* ii. 1, etc. ; *Lycidas*, 79 ; *Comus*, 219 ; *P. L.* iii. 550 ; iv. 645, 653, etc.

ETON COLLEGE.

ODE ON A DISTANT PROSPECT OF ETON COLLEGE.

THIS, as Mason informs us, was the first English* production of Gray's that appeared in print. It was published, in folio, in 1747 ; and appeared again in Dodsley's *Collection*, vol. ii. p. 267, without the name of the author.

Hazlitt (*Lectures on English Poets*) says of this Ode: " It is more mechanical and commonplace [than the *Elegy*] ; but it touches on certain strings about the heart, that vibrate in unison with it to our latest breath. No one ever passes by Windsor's ' stately heights,' or sees the distant spires of Eton College below, without thinking of Gray. He deserves that we should think of him ; for he thought of others, and turned a trembling, ever-watchful ear to ' the still sad music of humanity.' "

The writer in the *North American Review* (vol. xcvi.), after referring to the publication of this Ode, which, " according to the custom of the time, was judiciously swathed in folio," adds :

---

* A Latin poem by him, a " Hymeneal " on the Prince of Wales's Marriage, had appeared in the *Cambridge Collection* in 1736.

"About this time Gray's portrait was painted, at Walpole's request; and on the paper which he is represented as holding, Walpole wrote the title of the Ode, with a line from Lucan:

'Nec licuit populis parvum te, Nile, videre.'

The poem met with very little attention until it was republished in 1751, with a few other of his Odes. Gray, in speaking of it to Walpole, in connection with the Ode to Spring, merely says that to him 'the latter seems not worse than the former.' But the former has always been the greater favourite—perhaps more from the matter than the manner. It is the expression of the memories, the thoughts, and the feelings which arise unbidden in the mind of the man as he looks once more on the scenes of his boyhood. He feels a new youth in the presence of those old joys. But the old friends are not there. Generations have come and gone, and an unknown race now frolic in boyish glee. His sad, prophetic eye cannot help looking into the future, and comparing these careless joys with the inevitable ills of life. Already he sees the fury passions in wait for their little victims. They seem present to him, like very demons. Our language contains no finer, more graphic personifications than these almost tangible shapes. Spenser is more circumstantial, Collins more vehement, but neither is more real. Though but outlines in miniature, they are as distinct as Dutch art. Every epithet is a lifelike picture; not a word could be changed without destroying the tone of the whole. At last the musing poet asks himself, *Cui bono?* Why thus borrow trouble from the future? Why summon so soon the coming locusts, to poison before their time the glad waters of youth?

> 'Yet ah! why should they know their fate,
> Since sorrow never comes too late,
> And happiness too quickly flies?
> Thought would destroy their paradise.
> No more;—where ignorance is bliss,
> 'Tis folly to be wise.'

So feeling and the want of feeling come together for once in the moral. The gay Roman satirist—the apostle of indifferentism—reaches the same goal, though he has travelled a different road. To Thaliarchus he says:

> 'Quid sit futurum cras, fuge quaerere: et
> Quem Fors dierum cumque dabit, lucro
> Appone.'

The same easy-going philosophy of life forms the key-note of the Ode to Leuconoë:

> 'Carpe diem, quam minimum credula postero;'

of that to Quinctius Hirpinus:

> 'Quid aeternis minorem
> Consiliis animum fatigas?'

of that to Pompeius Grosphus:

> 'Laetus in praesens animus, quod ultra est,
> Oderit curare.'

And so with many others. 'Take no thought of the morrow.'"

Wakefield translates the Greek motto, "Man is an abundant subject of calamity."

2. *That crown the watery glade.* Cf. Pope, *Windsor Forest*, 128: "And lonely woodcocks haunt the watery glade."

4. *Her Henry's holy shade.* Henry the Sixth, founder of the college. Cf. *The Bard*, ii. 3: "the meek usurper's holy head;" Shakes. *Rich. III.* v. 1: "Holy King Henry;" *Id.* iv. 4: "When holy Harry died." The king, though never canonized, was regarded as a saint.

5. *And ye.* Ye "towers;" that is, of Windsor Castle. Cf. Thomson, *Summer*, 1412:

> "And now to where
> Majestic Windsor lifts his princely brow."

8. *Whose turf, whose shade, whose flowers among.* "That is, the *turf* of whose *lawn*, the *shade* of whose *groves*, the *flowers* of whose *mead*" (Wakefield). Cf. *Hamlet*, iii. 1: "The courtier's, soldier's, scholar's eye, tongue, sword."

In Anglo-Saxon and Early English prepositions were often placed after their objects. In the Elizabethan period the transposition of the weaker prepositions was not allowed, except in the compounds *whereto, herewith,* etc. (cf. the Latin *quocum, secum*), but the longer forms were still, though rarely, transposed (see *Shakes. Gr.* 203); and in more recent writers this latter license is extremely rare. Even the use of the preposition after the relative, which was very common in Shakespeare's day, is now avoided, except in colloquial style.

9. *The hoary Thames.* The river-god is pictured in the old classic fashion. Cf. Milton, *Lycidas*, 103: "Next Camus, reverend sire, went footing slow." See also quotation from Dryden in note on 21 below.

THE RIVER-GOD TIBER.

10. *His silver-winding way.* Cf. Thomson, *Summer*, 1425 : "The matchless vale of Thames, Fair-winding up," etc.

12. *Ah, fields belov'd in vain!* Mitford remarks that this expression has been considered obscure, and adds the following explanation : "The poem is written in the character of one who contemplates this life as a scene of misfortune and sorrow, from whose fatal power the brief sunshine of youth is supposed to be exempt. The fields are *beloved* as the scene of youthful pleasures, and as affording the promise of happiness to come ; but this promise never was fulfilled. Fate, which dooms man to misery, soon overclouded these opening prospects of delight. That is in vain beloved which does not realize the expectations it held out. No fruit but that of disappointment has followed the blossoms of a thoughtless hope."

13. *Where once my careless childhood stray'd.* Wakefield cites Thomson, *Winter*, 6 :

> "with frequent foot
> Pleas'd have I, in my cheerful morn of life,
> When nurs'd by careless Solitude I liv'd,
> And sung of Nature with unceasing joy,
> Pleas'd have I wander'd," etc.

15. *That from ye blow.* In Early English *ye* is nominative, *you* accusative (objective). This distinction, though observed in our version of the Bible, was disregarded by Elizabethan writers (*Shakes. Gr.* 236), as it has occasionally been by the poets even to our own day. Cf. Shakes. *Hen. VIII.* iii. 1 : "The more shame for ye ; holy men I thought ye ;" Milton, *Comus*, 216 : "I see ye visibly," etc. Dryden, in a couplet quoted by Guest, uses both forms in the same line :

> "What gain you by forbidding it to tease ye?
> It now can neither trouble *you* nor please *ye*."

19. Gray quotes Dryden, *Fable on Pythag. Syst.* : "And bees their honey redolent of spring."

21. *Say, father Thames*, etc. This invocation is taken from Green's *Grotto* :

> "Say, father Thames, whose gentle pace
> Gives leave to view, what beauties grace
> Your flowery banks, if you have seen."

Cf. Dryden, *Annus Mirabilis*, st. 232 : "Old father Thames raised up his reverend head."

Dr. Johnson, in his hypercritical comments on this Ode, says : "His supplication to Father Thames, to tell him who drives the hoop or tosses the ball, is useless and puerile. Father Thames has no better means of knowing than himself." To which Mitford replies by asking, "Are we by this rule to judge the following passage in the twentieth chapter of *Rasselas?* 'As they were sitting together, the princess cast her eyes on the river that flowed before her : "Answer," said she, "great Father of Waters, thou that rollest thy floods through eighty nations, to the invocation of the daughter of thy native king. Tell me, if thou waterest, through all thy course, a single habitation from which thou dost not hear the murmurs of complaint."'"

23. *Margent green.* Cf. *Comus,* 232 : " By slow Mæander's margent green."

24. Cf. Pope, *Essay on Man,* iii. 233 : " To Virtue, in the paths of Pleasure, trod."

26. *Thy glassy wave.* Cf. *Comus,* 861 : " Under the glassy, cool, translucent wave."

27. *The captive linnet.* The adjective is redundant and " proleptic," as the bird must be " enthralled " before it can be called " captive."

28. In the MS. this line reads, " To chase the hoop's illusive speed," which seems to us better than the revised form in the text.

30. Cf. Pope, *Dunciad,* iv. 592 : " The senator at cricket urge the ball."

37. Cf. Cowley, *Ode to Hobbes,* iv. 7 : " Till unknown regions it descries."

40. *A fearful joy.* Wakefield quotes *Matt.* xxviii. 8 and *Psalms* ii. 11. Cf. Virgil, *Æn.* i. 513 :

> "Obstupuit simul ipse simul perculsus Achates
> Laetitiaque metuque."

See also *Lear,* v. 3 : " 'Twixt two extremes of passion, joy and grief."

44. Cf. Pope, *Eloisa,* 209 : " Eternal sunshine of the spotless mind ;" and *Essay on Man,* iv. 168 : " The soul's calm sunshine, and the heart-felt joy."

45. *Buxom.* Used here in its modern sense. It originally meant pliant, flexible, yielding (from A. S. *búgan,* to bow) ; then, gay, frolicsome, lively ; and at last it became associated with the " cheerful comeliness " of vigorous health. Chaucer has " buxom to ther lawe," and Spenser *(State of Ireland),* " more tractable and buxome to his government." Cf. also *F. Q.* i. 11, 37 : " the buxome aire ;" an expression which Milton uses twice *(P. L.* ii. 842, v. 270). In *L'Allegro,* 24 : " So buxom, blithe, and debonaire ;" the only other instance in which he uses the word, it means sprightly or " free " (as in " Come thou goddess, fair and free," a few lines before). Cf. Shakes. *Pericles,* i. prologue :

> "So buxom, blithe, and full of face,
> As heaven had lent her all his grace."

The word occurs nowhere else in Shakes. except *Hen. V.* iii. 6 : " Of buxom valour ;" that is, lively valour.

Dr. Johnson appears to have had in mind the original meaning of *buxom* in his comment on this passage : " His epithet *buxom health* is not elegant ; he seems not to understand the word."

47. *Lively cheer.* Cf. Spenser, *Shep. Kal.* Apr. : " In either cheeke depeincten lively chere ;" Milton, *Ps.* lxxxiv. 27 : " With joy and gladsome cheer."

49. Wakefield quotes Milton, *P. L.* v. 3 :

> "When Adam wak'd, so custom'd ; for his sleep
> Was airy light, from pure digestion bred,
> And temperate vapours bland."

51. *Regardless of their doom.* Collins, in the *first manuscript* of his *Ode on the Death of Col. Ross,* has

> " E'en now, regardful of his doom,
> Applauding Honour haunts his tomb."*

55. *Yet see,* etc. Mitford cites Broome, *Ode on Melancholy :*

> "While round stern ministers of fate,
> Pain and Disease and Sorrow, wait ;"

and Otway, *Alcibiades,* v. 2 : " Then enter, ye grim ministers of fate."
See also *Progress of Poesy,* ii. 1 : " Man's feeble race," etc.

59. *Murtherous.* The obsolete spelling of *murderous,* still used in
Gray's time.

61. *The fury Passions.* The passions, fierce and cruel as the mythical
Furies. Cf. Pope, *Essay on Man,* iii. 167 : " The fury Passions from that
blood began."

66. Mitford quotes Spenser, *F. Q. :*

> "But gnawing Jealousy out of their sight,
> Sitting alone, his bitter lips did bite."

68. Wakefield quotes Milton, *Sonnet to Mr. Lawes :* "With praise
enough for Envy to look wan."

69. *Grim-visag'd, comfortless Despair.* Cf. Shakes. *Rich. III.* i. 1 :
"Grim-visag'd War ;" and *C. of E.* v. 1 : "grim and comfortless Despair."

76. *Unkindness' altered eye.* "An ungraceful elision " of the possessive
inflection, as Mason calls it. *Cf. Dryden, *Hind and Panther,* iii. : " Affected Kindness with an alter'd face."

79. Gray quotes Dryden, *Pal. and Arc. :* " Madness laughing in his
ireful mood." Cf. Shakes. *Hen. VI.* iv. 2 : " But rather moody mad ;"
and iii. 1 : "Moody discontented fury."

81. *The vale of years.* Cf. *Othello,* iii. 3 : "Declin'd Into the vale of
years."

82. *Grisly.* Not to be confounded with *grizzly.* See Wb.

83. *The painful family of death.* Cf. Pope, *Essay on Man,* ii. 118 :
" Hate, Fear, and Grief, the family of Pain ;" and Dryden, *State of Innocence,* v. 1 : "With all the numerous family of Death." On the whole
passage cf. Milton, *P. L.* xi. 477-493. See also Virgil, *Æn.* vi. 275.

86. *That every labouring sinew strains.* An example of the "correspondence of sound with sense." As Pope says (*Essay on Criticism,* 371),

> "The line too labours, and the words move slow."

90. *Slow-consuming Age.* Cf. Shenstone, *Love and Honour :* " His slow-
consuming fires."

95. As Wakefield remarks, we meet with the same thought in *Comus,*
359 :

> "Peace, brother, be not over-exquisite
> To cast the fashion of uncertain evils ;
> For grant they be so, while they rest unknown
> What need a man forestall his date of grief,
> And run to meet what he would most avoid ?"

---

* Mitford gives the first line as " E'en now, *regardless* of his doom ;" and just below,
on verse 61, he makes the line from Pope read, " The fury Passions from that *flood* began."
We have verified his quotations as far as possible, and have corrected scores of errors
in them. Quite likely there are some errors in those we have not been able to verify.

97. *Happiness too swiftly flies.*   Perhaps a reminiscence of Virgil, *Geo.*
iii. 66 :

> "Optima quaeque dies miseris mortalibus aevi
> Prima fugit."

98. *Thought would destroy their paradise.*   Wakefield quotes Sophocles,
Ajax, 554 : Ἐν τῷ φρονεῖν γὰρ μηδὲν ἥδιστος βίος ("Absence of thought
is prime felicity ").

99. Cf. Prior, *Ep. to Montague*, st. 9 :

> "From ignorance our comfort flows,
> The only wretched are the wise."

and Davenant, *Just Italian :* "Since knowledge is but sorrow's spy, it
is not safe to know."

WINDSOR CASTLE, FROM THE END OF THE LONG WALK.

ΟΙΚΟΥΜΕΝΗ ΧΡΟΝΟΣΙΛΙΑΣ ΟΔΥΣΣΕΙΑ ΟΜΗΡΟΣ ΜΥΘΟΣ

HOMER ENTHRONED.

THE PROGRESS OF POESY.

THIS Ode, as we learn from one of Gray's letters to Walpole, was finished, with the exception of a few lines, in 1755. It was not published until 1757, when it appeared with *The Bard* in a quarto volume, which was the first issue of Walpole's press at Strawberry Hill. In one of his letters Walpole writes: "I send you two copies of a very honourable opening of my press—two amazing odes of Mr. Gray. They are Greek, they are Pindaric, they are sublime, consequently I fear a little obscure; the second particularly, by the confinement of the measure and the nature of prophetic vision, is mysterious. I could not persuade him to add more notes." In another letter Walpole says: "I found Gray in town last week; he had brought his two odes to be printed. I snatched them out of Dodsley's hands, and they are to be the first-fruits of my press." The title-page of the volume is as follows:

ODES | BY | MR. GRAY. | ΦΩΝΑΝΤΑ ΣΥΝΕΤΟΙΣΙ—PINDAR, Olymp. II. | PRINTED AT STRAWBERRY-HILL, | for R. and J. DODSLEY in Pall-Mall. | MDCCLVII.

Both Odes were coldly received at first. "Even my friends," writes Gray, in a letter to Hurd, Aug. 25, 1757, "tell me they do not *succeed*,

and write me moving topics of consolation on that head. In short, I
have heard of nobody but an Actor [Garrick] and a Doctor of Divinity
[Warburton] that profess their esteem for them. Oh yes, a Lady of
quality (a friend of Mason's) who is a great reader. She knew there was
a compliment to Dryden, but never suspected there was anything said
about Shakespeare or Milton, till it was explained to her, and wishes
that there had been titles prefixed to tell what they were about."* In a
letter to Dr. Wharton, dated Aug. 17, 1757, he says : "I hear we are not
at all popular. The great objection is obscurity, nobody knows what we
would be at. One man (a Peer) I have been told of, that thinks the last
stanza of the 2d Ode relates to Charles the First and Oliver Cromwell ;
in short, the Συνετοί appear to be still fewer than even I expected." A
writer in the *Critical Review* thought that "Æolian lyre" meant the Æolian
harp. Coleman the elder and Robert Lloyd wrote parodies entitled Odes
to Obscurity and Oblivion. Gray finally had to add explanatory notes,
though he intimates that his readers ought not to have needed them.†

"The metre of these Odes is constructed on Greek models. It is not
uniform but symmetrical. The nine stanzas of each ode form three groups.
A slight examination will show that the 1st, 4th, and 7th stanzas are exactly inter-correspondent ; so the 2d, 5th, and 8th ; and so the remaining
three. The technical Greek names for these three parts were στροφή
(strophe), ἀντιστροφή (antistrophe), and ἐπωδός (epodos)—the Turn, the
Counter-turn, and the After-song—names derived from the theatre ; the
Turn denoting the movement of the Chorus from one side of the ὀρχηστρά
(orchestra), or Dance-stage, to the other, the Counter-turn the reverse
movement, the After-song something sung after two such movements.
Odes thus constructed were called by the Greeks Epodic. Congreve is
said to have been the first who so constructed English odes. This system
cannot be said to have prospered with us. Perhaps no English ear would
instinctively recognize that correspondence between distant parts which
is the secret of it. Certainly very many readers of *The Progress of Poesy*
are wholly unconscious of any such harmony" (Hales).

---

* Forster remarks that Gray might have added to the admirers of the Odes "the poor
monthly critic of *The Dunciad*"—Oliver Goldsmith, then beginning his London career
as a bookseller's hack. In a review of the Odes in the *London Monthly Review* for Sept.,
1757, after citing certain passages of *The Bard*, he says that they "will give as much
pleasure to those who relish this species of composition as anything that has hitherto appeared in our language, the odes of Dryden himself not excepted."

† In a foot-note he says: "When the author first published this and the following Ode,
he was advised, even by his friends, to subjoin some few explanatory notes ; but had too
much respect for the understanding of his readers to take that liberty."

In a letter to Beattie, dated Feb. 1, 1768, referring to the new edition of his poems, he
says: "As to the notes, I do it out of spite, because the public did not understand the two
Odes (which I have called Pindaric), though the first was not very dark, and the second
alluded to a few common facts to be found in any sixpenny history of England, by way of
question and answer, for the use of children." And in a letter to Walpole, Feb. 25, 1768,
he says he has added "certain little Notes, partly from justice (to acknowledge the debt
where I had borrowed anything), partly from ill temper, just to tell the gentle reader that
Edward I. was not Oliver Cromwell, nor Queen Elizabeth the Witch of Endor."

Mr. Fox, afterwards Lord Holland, said that "if the Bard recited his Ode only *once* to
Edward, he was sure he could not understand it." When this was told to Gray, he said,
"If he had recited it twenty times, Edward would not have been a bit wiser ; but that was
no reason why Mr. Fox should not."

ALCÆUS AND SAPPHO. FROM A PAINTING ON A VASE.

1. *Awake, Æolian lyre.* The blunder of the Critical Reviewers who supposed the "harp of Æolus" to be meant led Gray to insert this note: "Pindar styles his own poetry with its musical accompaniments, Αἰολὶς μολπή, Αἰολίδες χορδαί, Αἰολίδων πνοαὶ αὐλῶν, Æolian song, Æolian strings, the breath of the Æolian flute."

Cf. Cowley, *Ode of David:* "Awake, awake, my lyre!" Gray himself quotes *Ps.* lvii. 8. The first reading of the line in the MS. was, "Awake, my lyre: my glory, wake." Gray also adds the following note: "The subject and simile, as usual with Pindar, are united. The various sources of poetry, which gives life and lustre to all it touches, are here described; its quiet majestic progress enriching every subject (otherwise dry and barren) with a pomp of diction and luxuriant harmony of numbers; and its more rapid and irresistible course, when swollen and hurried away by the conflict of tumultuous passions."

2. *And give to rapture.* The first reading of the MS. was "give to transport."

3. *Helicon's harmonious springs.* In the mountain range of Helicon, in Bœotia, there were two fountains sacred to the Muses, Aganippe and Hippocrene, of which the former was the more famous.

7. Cf. Pope, *Hor. Epist.* ii. 2, 171:

> "Pour the full tide of eloquence along,
>   Serenely pure, and yet divinely strong;"

and *Ode on St. Cecilia's Day*, 11:

> "The deep, majestic, solemn organs blow;"

also Thomson, *Liberty*, ii. 257:

> "In thy full language speaking mighty things,
>   Like a clear torrent close, or else diffus'd
> A broad majestic stream, and rolling on
>   Through all the winding harmony of sound."

9. Cf. Shenstone, *Inscr.:* "Verdant vales and fountains bright;" also Virgil, *Geo.* i. 96: "Flava Ceres;" and Homer, *Il.* v. 499: ξανθὴ Δημήτηρ.

10. *Rolling.* Spelled "rowling" in the 1st and other early editions.

Amain. Cf. *Lycidas*, 111: "The golden opes, the iron shuts amain;" *P. L.* ii. 165: "when we fled amain," etc. Also Shakes. *Temp.* iv. 1: "Her peacocks fly amain," etc. The word means literally *with main* (which we still use in "might and main"), that is, with force or strength. Cf. Horace, *Od.* iv. 2, 8: "Immensusque ruit profundo Pindarus ore."

11. The first MS. reading was, "With torrent rapture see it pour."

12. Cf. Dryden, *Virgil's Geo.* i.: "And rocks the bellowing voice of boiling seas resound;" Pope, *Iliad:* "Rocks rebellow to the roar."

13. "Power of harmony to calm the turbulent sallies of the soul. The thoughts are borrowed from the first Pythian of Pindar" (Gray).

14. *Solemn-breathing airs.* Cf. *Comus*, 555: "a soft and solemn-breathing sound."

15. *Enchanting shell.* That is, lyre; alluding to the myth of the origin of the instrument, which Mercury was said to have made from the shell of a tortoise. Cf. Collins, *Passions*, 3: "The Passions oft, to hear her shell," etc.

17. *On Thracia's hills.* Thrace was one of the chief seats of the worship of Mars. Cf. Ovid, *Ars Am.* ii. 588: "Mars Thracen occupat." See also Virgil, *Æn.* iii. 35, etc.

19. *His thirsty lance.* Cf. Spenser, *F. Q.* i. 5, 15: "his thristy [thirsty] blade."

20. Gray says, "This is a weak imitation of some beautiful lines in the same ode;" that is, in "the first Pythian of Pindar," referred to in the note on 13. The passage is an address to the lyre, and is translated by Wakefield thus:

> "On Jove's imperial rod the king of birds
> Drops down his flagging wings; thy thrilling sounds
> Soothe his fierce beak, and pour a sable cloud
> Of slumber on his eyelids: up he lifts
> His flexile back, shot by thy piercing darts.
> Mars smooths his rugged brow, and nerveless **drops**
> His lance, relenting at the choral song."

21. *The feather'd king.* Cf. Shakes. *Phœnix and Turtle:*

> "Every fowl of tyrant wing,
> Save the eagle, feather'd king."

23. *Dark clouds.* The first reading of MS. was "black clouds."

24. *The terror.* This is the reading of the first ed. and also of that of 1768. Most of the modern eds. have "terrors."

25. "Power of harmony to produce all the graces of motion in the body" (Gray).

26. *Temper'd.* Modulated, "set." Cf. *Lycidas*, 33: "Tempered to the oaten flute;" Fletcher, *Purple Island:* "Tempering their sweetest notes unto thy lay," etc.

27. *O'er Idalia's velvet-green. Idalia* appears to be used for *Idalium*, which was a town in Cyprus, and a favourite seat of Venus, who was sometimes called *Idalia.* Pope likewise uses *Idalia* for the place, in his *First Pastoral*, 65: "Celestial Venus haunts Idalia's groves."

Dr. Johnson finds fault with *velvet-green*, apparently supposing it to be a compound of Gray's own making. But Young had used it in his *Love of Fame :* " She rears her flowers, and spreads her velvet-green." It is also among the expressions of Pope which are ridiculed in the *Alexandriad.*

29. *Cytherea* was a name of Venus, derived from *Cythera*, an island in the Ægean Sea, one of the favourite residences of Aphrodite, or Venus. Cf. Virgil, *Æn.* i. 680 : "super alta Cythera Aut super Idalium, sacrata sede," etc.

30. *With antic Sports.* This is the reading of the 1st ed. and also of the ed. of 1768. Some eds. have "sport."

Antic is the same word as *antique.* The association between what is old or old-fashioned and what is odd, fantastic, or grotesque is obvious enough. Cf. Milton, *Il Pens.* 158 : " With antick pillars massy-proof." In *S. A.* 1325 he uses the word as a noun : " Jugglers and dancers, anticks, mummers, mimicks." Shakes. makes it a verb in *A. and C.* ii. 7 : " the wild disguise hath almost Antick'd us all."

31. Cf. Thomson, *Spring*, 835 : " In friskful glee Their frolics play."

32, 33. Cf. Virgil, *Æn.* v. 580 foll.

35. Gray quotes Homer, *Od.* ix. 265 : μαρμαρυγὰς Ͽηεῖτο ποδῶν Ͽαύμαζε δὲ Ͽυμῷ. Cf. Catullus's "fulgentem plantam." See also Thomson, *Spring*, 158 : " the many-twinkling leaves Of aspin tall."

36. *Slow-melting strains,* etc. Cf. a poem by Barton Booth, published in 1733 :

> " Now to a slow and melting air she moves,
> So like in air, in shape, in mien,
> She passes for the Paphian queen ;
> The Graces all around her play,
> The wondering gazers die away ;
> Whether her easy body bend,
> Or her fair bosom heave with sighs ;
> Whether her graceful arms extend,
> Or gently fall, or slowly rise ;
> Or returning or advancing,
> Swimming round, or sidelong glancing,
> Strange force of motion that subdues the soul."

37. Cf. Dryden, *Flower and Leaf,* 191 : " For wheresoe'er she turn'd her face, they bow'd."

39. Cf. Virgil, *Æn.* i. 405 : " Incessu patuit dea." The gods were represented as gliding or sailing along without moving their feet.

41. *Purple light of love.* Cf. Virgil, *Æn.* i. 590 : "lumenque juventae Purpureum." Gray quotes Phrynichus, *apud* Athenæum :

> λάμπει δ' ἐπὶ πορφυρέῃσι
> παρείῃσι φῶς ἔρωτος.

See also Dryden, *Brit. Red.* 133 : " and her own purple light."

42. " To compensate the real and imaginary ills of life, the Muse was given to mankind by the same Providence that sends the day by its cheerful presence to dispel the gloom and terrors of the night " (Gray).

43 foll. See on *Eton Coll.* 83. Cf. Horace, *Od.* i. 3, 29-33.

46. *Fond complaint.* Foolish complaint. Cf. Shakes. *M. of V.* iii. 3 :

> "I do wonder,
> Thou naughty gaoler, that thou art so fond
> To come abroad with him at his request;"

Milton, *S. A.* 812 : "fond and reasonless," etc.   This appears to be the original meaning of the word.   In Wiclif's Bible, 1 *Cor.* i. 27, we have "the thingis that ben *fonnyd* of the world."   In *Twelfth Night*, ii. 2, the word is used as a verb=dote :

> "And I, poor monster, fond as much on him,
> As she, mistaken, seems to dote on me."

49. Hurd quotes Cowley:

> "Night and her ugly subjects thou dost fright,
> And 'Sleep, the lazy owl of night ;
> Asham'd and fearful to appear,
> They screen their horrid shapes with the black hemisphere."

Wakefield cites Milton, *Hymn on Nativity*, 233 foll. : "The flocking shadows pale," etc.   See also *P. R.* iv. 419-431.

50. *Birds of boding cry.*   Cf. Green's *Grotto :* "news the boding night-birds tell."

52. Gray refers to Cowley, *Brutus :*

> "One would have thought 't had heard the morning crow,
> Or seen her well-appointed star.
> Come marching up the eastern hill afar."

The following variations on 52 and 53 are found in the MS. :

> Till fierce Hyperion from afar
> Pours on their scatter'd rear, ⎫
> Hurls at   "   flying   "   ⎬ his glittering shafts of war.
> "   o'er " scatter'd "   ⎭
> "   "   "   shadowy "
> Till   "   "   "   " from far
> Hyperion hurls around his, etc.

The accent of *Hyperion* is properly on the penult, which is long in quantity, but the English poets, with rare exceptions, have thrown it back upon the antepenult.   It is thus in the six instances in which Shakes. uses the word : e. g. *Hamlet*, iii. 4 : "Hyperion's curls ; the front of Jove himself."   The word does not occur in Milton.   It is correctly accented by Drummond (of Hawthornden), *Wand. Muses :*

> "That Hyperion far beyond his bed
> Doth see our lions ramp, our roses spread ;"

by West, *Pindar's Ol.* viii. 22 :

> "Then Hyperion's son, pure fount of day,
> Did to his children the strange tale reveal ;"

also by Akenside, and by the author of the old play *Fuimus Troes* (A.D. 1633) :

> "Blow, gentle Africus,
> Play on our poops when Hyperion's son
> Shall couch in west."

Hyperion was a Titan, the father of Helios (the Sun), Selene (the Moon), and Eos (the Dawn).   He was represented with the attributes of beauty and splendor afterwards ascribed to Apollo. His "glittering shafts" are of course the sunbeams, the "lucida tela diei" of Lucretius. Cf. a very beautiful description of the dawn in Lowell's *Above and Below:*

> "'Tis from these heights alone your eyes
> The advancing spears of day can see,
> Which o'er the eastern hill-tops rise,
> To break your long captivity."

We may quote also his *Vision of Sir Launfal:*

> "It seemed the dark castle had gathered all
> Those shafts the fierce sun had shot over its wall
> In his siege of three hundred summers long," etc.

54. Gray's note here is as follows : "Extensive influence of poetic genius over the remotest and most uncivilized nations ; its connection with liberty and the virtues that naturally attend on it. [See the Erse, Norwegian, and Welsh fragments ; the Lapland and American songs.]" He also quotes Virgil, *Æn.* vi. 796 : "Extra anni solisque vias," and Petrarch, *Canz.* 2 : "Tutta lontana dal camin del sole." Cf. also Dryden, *Thren. August.* 353 : "Out of the solar walk and Heaven's highway ;" *Ann. Mirab.* st. 160 : "Beyond the year, and out of Heaven's highway ;" *Brit. Red.:* "Beyond the sunny walks and circling year ;" also Pope, *Essay on Man,* i. 102 : "Far as the solar walk and milky way."

56. *Twilight gloom.* Wakefield quotes Milton, *Hymn on Nativ.* 188 : "The nymphs in twilight shade of tangled thickets mourn."

57. Wakefield says, "It almost chills one to read this verse." The MS. variations are "buried native's" and "chill abode."

60. *Repeat* [*their chiefs,* etc.]. Sing of them again and again.

61. *In loose numbers,* etc. Cf. Milton, *L'All.* 133 :

> "Or sweetest Shakespeare, Fancy's child,
> Warble his native wood-notes wild ;"

and Horace, *Od.* iv. 2, 11 :

> "numerisque fertur
> Lege solutis."

62. *Their feather-cinctur'd chiefs.* Cf. *P. L.* ix. 1115 :

> "Such of late
> Columbus found the American, so girt
> With feather'd cincture."

64. *Glory pursue.* Wakefield remarks that this use of a plural verb after the first of a series of subjects is in Pindar's manner. Warton compares Homer, *Il.* v. 774 :

> ἧχι ῥοὰς Σιμόεις συμβάλλετον ἠδὲ Σκάμανδρος.

Dugald Stewart (*Philos. of Human Mind*) says : "I cannot help remarking the effect of the solemn and uniform flow of verse in this exquisite stanza, in retarding the pronunciation of the reader, so as to arrest his attention to every successive picture, till it has time to produce its proper impression."

65. *Freedom's holy flame.* Cf. Akenside, *Pleas. of Imag.* i. 468 : "Love's holy flame."

H

THE VALE OF TEMPE.

66. "Progress of Poetry from Greece to Italy, and from Italy to England. Chaucer was not unacquainted with the writings of Dante or of Petrarch. The Earl of Surrey and Sir Thomas Wyatt had travelled in Italy, and formed their taste there; Spenser imitated the Italian writers; Milton improved on them : but this school expired soon after the Restoration, and a new one arose on the French model, which has subsisted ever since " (Gray).

Delphi's steep. Cf. Milton, *Hymn on Nativ.* 178 : "the steep of Delphos ;" *P. L.* i. 517 : "the Delphian cliff." Both Shakes. and Milton prefer the mediæval form *Delphos* to the more usual *Delphi.* Delphi was at the foot of the southern uplands of Parnassus which end "in a precipitous cliff, 2000 feet high, rising to a double peak named the Phædriades, from their glittering appearance as they faced the rays of the sun " (Smith's *Anc. Geog.*).

67. *Isles,* etc. Cf. Byron :

"The isles of Greece, the isles of Greece !
    Where burning Sappho loved and sung," etc. ·

68. *Ilissus.* This river, rising on the northern slope of Hymettus, flows through the east side of Athens.

69. *Mæander's amber waves.* Cf. Milton, *P. L.* iii. 359 : "Rolls o'er Elysian flowers her amber stream ;" *P. R.* iii. 288 : "There Susa by Choaspes, amber stream." See also Virgil, *Geo.* iii. 520 : " Purior electro campum petit amnis." Callimachus (*Cer.* 29) has ἀλέκτρινον ὕδωρ.

70. Ovid, *Met.* viii. 162, describes the Mæander thus :

> "Non secus ac liquidis Phrygiis Maeandros in arvis
> Ludit, et ambiguo lapsu refluitque fluitque."

Cf. also Virgil's description of the Mincius (*Geo.* iii. 15) :

> —"tardis ingens ubi flexibus errat
> Mincius."

"The first great metropolis of Hellenic intellectual life was Miletus on the Mæander. Thales, Anaximander, Anaximines, Cadmus, Hecatæus, etc., were all Milesians " (Hales).

71 foll. Cf. Milton, *Hymn on Nativ.* 181 :

> "The lonely mountains o'er,
> And the resounding shore,
> A voice of weeping heard and loud lament ;
> From haunted spring and dale,
> Edged with poplar pale,
> The parting Genius is with sighing sent :" etc.

75. *Hallowed fountain.* Cf. Virgil, *Ecl.* i. 53 : "fontes sacros."
76. The MS. has "Murmur'd a celestial sound."
80. *Vice that revels in her chains.* In his *Ode for Music*, 6, Gray has "Servitude that hugs her chain."
81. Hales quotes Collins, *Ode to Simplicity :*

> "While Rome could none esteem
> But Virtue's patriot theme,
> You lov'd her hills, and led her laureate band ;
> But staid to sing alone
> To one distinguish'd throne,
> And turn'd thy face, and fled her alter'd land."

84. *Nature's darling.* "Shakespeare" (Gray). Cf. Cleveland, *Poems :*

> "Here lies within this stony shade
> Nature's darling ; whom she made
> Her fairest model, her brief story,
> In him heaping all her glory."

On *green lap*, cf. Milton, *Song on May Morning :*

> "The flowery May, who from her green lap throws
> The yellow cowslip and the pale primrose."

85. *Lucid Avon.* Cf. Seneca, *Thyest.* 129 : "gelido flumine lucidus Alpheos."
86. *The mighty mother.* That is, Nature. Pope, in the *Dunciad*, i. 1, uses the same expression in a satirical way :

> "The Mighty Mother, and her Son, who brings
> The Smithfield Muses to the ear of kings,
> I sing."

See also Dryden, *Georgics*, i. 466 :

> "On the green turf thy careless limbs display,
> And celebrate the mighty mother's day."

87. *The dauntless child.* Cf. Horace, *Od.* iii. 4, 20 : "non sine dis animosus infans." Wakefield quotes Virgil, *Ecl.* iv. 60 : "Incipe, parve

puer, risu cognoscere matrem." Mitford points out that the identical expression occurs in Sandys's translation of Ovid, *Met.* iv. 515 :

> "the child
> Stretch'd forth its little arms, and on him smil'd."

See also Catullus, *In Nupt. Jun. et Manl.* 216 :

> "Torquatus volo parvulus
> Matris e gremio suae
> Porrigens teneras manus,
> Dulce rideat."

91. *These golden keys.* Cf. Young, *Resig.* :

> "Nature, which favours to the few
> All art beyond imparts,
> To him presented at his birth
> The key of human hearts."

Wakefield cites *Comus*, 12 :

> "Yet some there be, that with due steps aspire
> To lay their hands upon that golden key
> That opes the palace of eternity."

See also *Lycidas*, 110 :

> "Two massy keys he bore of metals twain ;
> The golden opes, the iron shuts amain."

93. *Of horror.* A MS. variation is "Of terror."
94. *Or ope the sacred source.* In a letter to Dr. Wharton, Sept. 7, 1757,
Gray mentions, among other criticisms upon this ode, that "Dr. Akenside
criticises opening a *source* with a *key*." But, as Mitford remarks, Akenside
himself in his *Ode on Lyric Poetry* has, "While I so late *unlock* thy purer
springs," and in his *Pleasures of Imagination*, "I *unlock* the *springs* of
ancient wisdom."
95. *Nor second he*, etc. "Milton" (Gray).
96, 97. Cf. Milton, *P. L.* vii. 12 :

> "Up led by thee,
> Into the heaven of heavens I have presumed,
> An earthly guest, and drawn empyreal air."

98. *The flaming bounds*, etc. Gray quotes Lucretius, i. 74 : "Flam-
mantia moenia mundi." Cf. also Horace, *Epist.* i. 14, 9 : "amat spatiis
obstantia rumpere claustra."
99. Gray quotes *Ezekiel* i. 20, 26, 28. See also Milton, *At a Solemn
Music*, 7 : "Aye sung before the sapphire-colour'd throne ;" *Il Pens.* 53 :
"the fiery-wheeled throne ;" *P. L.* vi. 758 :

> "Whereon a sapphire throne, inlaid with pure
> Amber, and colours of the showery arch ;"

and *id.* vi. 771 :

> "He on the wings of cherub rode sublime,
> On the crystalline sky, in sapphire throned."

101. *Blasted with excess of light.* Cf. *P. L.* iii. 380 : "Dark with ex-
cessive bright thy skirts appear."

102. Cf. Virgil, *Æn.* x. 746 : "in aeternam clauduntur lumina noctem," which Dryden translates, "And closed her lids at last in endless night." Gray quotes Homer, *Od.* viii. 64 :

Ὀφθαλμῶν μὲν ἄμερσες· δίδου δ' ἡδεῖαν ἀοιδήν.

103. Gray, according to Mason, "admired Dryden almost beyond bounds."*

105. "Meant to express the stately march and sounding energy of Dryden's rhymes" (Gray). Cf. Pope, *Imit. of Hor. Ep.* ii. 1, 267 :

> "Waller was smooth: but Dryden taught to join
> The varying verse, the full-resounding line,
> The long majestic march, and energy divine."

106. Gray quotes *Job* xxxix. 19 : "Hast thou clothed his neck with thunder ?"

108. *Bright-eyed.* The MS. has "full-plumed."

110. Gray quotes Cowley, *Prophet :* " Words that weep, and tears that speak."

Dugald Stewart remarks upon this line : "I have sometimes thought that Gray had in view the two different effects of words already described ; the effect of some in awakening the powers of conception and imagination ; and that of others in exciting associated emotions."

111. "We have had in our language no other odes of the sublime kind than that of Dryden on St. Cecilia's Day ; for Cowley (who had his merit) yet wanted judgment, style, and harmony, for such a task. That of Pope is not worthy of so great a man. Mr. Mason, indeed, of late days, has touched the true chords, and with a masterly hand, in some of his choruses ; above all in the last of *Caractacus :*

> 'Hark! heard ye not yon footstep dread!' etc." (Gray).

113. *Wakes thee now.* Cf. *Elegy*, 48 : "Or wak'd to ecstasy the living lyre."

115. "Διὸς πρὸς ὄρνιχα θεῖον. *Olymp.* ii. 159. Pindar compares himself to that bird, and his enemies to ravens that croak and clamour in vain below, while it pursues its flight, regardless of their noise" (Gray).

Cf. Spenser, *F. Q.* v. 4, 42 :

> "Like to an Eagle, in his kingly pride
> Soring through his wide Empire of the aire,
> To weather his brode sailes."

Cowley, in his translation of Horace, *Od.* iv. 2, calls Pindar "the Theban swan" ("Dircaeum cycnum") :

> "Lo! how the obsequious wind and swelling air
> The Theban Swan does upward bear."

117. *Azure deep of air.* Cf. Euripides, *Med.* 1294 : ἐς αἰθέρος βάθος ; and Lucretius, ii. 151 : "Aëris in magnum fertur mare." Cowley has

---

* In a journey through Scotland in 1765, Gray became acquainted with Beattie, to whom he commended the study of Dryden, adding that "if there was any excellence in his own numbers, he had learned it wholly from the great poet."

" Row through the trackless ocean of air ;" and Shakes. (*T. of A.* iv. 2), " this sea of air."

118, 119. The MS. reads :

> " Yet when they first were open'd on the day
> Before his visionary eyes would run.''

D. Stewart (*Philos. of Human Mind*) remarks that " Gray, in describing the infantine reveries of poetical genius, has fixed with exquisite judgment on that class of our conceptions which are derived from *visible* objects."

120. *With orient hues.* Cf. Milton, *P. L.* i. 546 : " with orient colours waving."

122. The MS. has " Yet never can he fear a vulgar fate."

123. Cf. K. Philips : " Still shew'd how much the good outshone the great."

We append, as a curiosity of criticism, Dr. Johnson's comments on this ode, from his *Lives of the Poets.* The Life of Gray has been called " the worst in the series," and perhaps this is the worst part of it :*

" My process has now brought me to the *wonderful* ' Wonder of Wonders,' the two Sister Odes, by which, though either vulgar ignorance or common-sense at first universally rejected them, many have been since persuaded to think themselves delighted. I am one of those that are willing to be pleased, and therefore would gladly find the meaning of the first stanza of ' The Progress of Poetry.'

" Gray seems in his rapture to confound the images of spreading sound and running water. A ' stream of music ' may be allowed ; but where does ' music,' however ' smooth and strong,' after having visited the ' verdant vales, roll down the steep amain,' so as that ' rocks and nodding groves rebellow to the roar ?' If this be said of music, it is nonsense ; if it be said of water, it is nothing to the purpose.

---

* Sir James Mackintosh well says of Johnson's criticisms : " Wherever understanding alone is sufficient for poetical criticism, the decisions of Johnson are generally right. But the beauties of poetry must be *felt* before their causes are investigated. There is a poetical sensibility, which in the progress of the mind becomes as distinct a power as a musical ear or a picturesque eye. Without a considerable degree of this sensibility, it is as vain for a man of the greatest understanding to speak of the higher beauties of poetry as it is for a blind man to speak of colours. To adopt the warmest sentiments of poetry, to realize its boldest imagery, to yield to every impulse of enthusiasm, to submit to the illusions of fancy, to retire with the poet into his ideal worlds, were dispositions wholly foreign from the worldly sagacity and stern shrewdness of Johnson. As in his judgment of life and character, so in his criticism on poetry, he was a sort of Free-thinker. He suspected the refined of affectation, he rejected the enthusiastic as absurd, and he took it for granted that the mysterious was unintelligible. He came into the world when the school of Dryden and Pope gave the law to English poetry. In that school he had himself learned to be a lofty and vigorous declaimer in harmonious verse ; beyond that school his unforced admiration perhaps scarcely soared ; and his highest effort of criticism was accordingly the noble panegyric on Dryden."

W. H. Prescott, the historian, also remarks that Johnson, as a critic, " was certainly deficient in sensibility to the more delicate, the minor beauties of poetic sentiment. He analyzes verse in the cold-blooded spirit of a chemist, until all the aroma which constituted its principal charm escapes in the decomposition. By this kind of process, some of the finest fancies of the Muse, the lofty dithyrambics of Gray, the ethereal effusions of Collins, and of Milton too, are rendered sufficiently vapid."

" The second stanza, exhibiting Mars's car and Jove's eagle, is unworthy of further notice. Criticism disdains to chase a schoolboy to his common-places.

" To the third it may likewise be objected that it is drawn from mythology, though such as may be more easily assimilated to real life. Idalia's 'velvet-green' has something of cant. An epithet or metaphor drawn from Nature ennobles Art; an epithet or metaphor drawn from Art degrades Nature. Gray is too fond of words arbitrarily compounded. 'Many-twinkling' was formerly censured as not analogical; we may say 'many-spotted,' but scarcely 'many-spotting.' This stanza, however, has something pleasing.

" Of the second ternary of stanzas, the first endeavours to tell something, and would have told it, had it not been crossed by Hyperion; the second describes well enough the universal prevalence of poetry; but I am afraid that the conclusion will not arise from the premises. The caverns of the North and the plains of Chili are not the residences of 'Glory and generous Shame.' But that Poetry and Virtue go always together is an opinion so pleasing that I can forgive him who resolves to think it true.

" The third stanza sounds big with 'Delphi,' and 'Ægean,' and 'Ilissus,' and 'Mæander,' and with 'hallowed fountains,' and 'solemn sound;' but in all Gray's odes there is a kind of cumbrous splendour which we wish away. His position is at last false : in the time of Dante and Petrarch, from whom we derive our first school of poetry, Italy was overrun by 'tyrant power' and 'coward vice;' nor was our state much better when we first borrowed the Italian arts.

" Of the third ternary, the first gives a mythological birth of Shakespeare. What is said of that mighty genius is true; but it is not said happily : the real effects of this poetical power are put out of sight by the pomp of machinery. Where truth is sufficient to fill the mind, fiction is worse than useless ; the counterfeit debases the genuine.

" His account of Milton's blindness, if we suppose it caused by study in the formation of his poem, a supposition surely allowable, is poetically true and happily imagined. But the *car* of Dryden, with his *two coursers*, has nothing in it peculiar ; it is a car in which any other rider may be placed."

ΠΙΝΔΑΡΟΣ

PINDAR.

EDWARD I.

THE BARD.

"THIS ode is founded on a tradition current in Wales that Edward the First, when he completed the conquest of that country, ordered all the bards that fell into his hands to be put to death" (Gray).

The original argument of the ode, as Gray had set it down in his commonplace-book, was as follows: "The army of Edward I., as they march through a deep valley, and approach Mount Snowdon, are suddenly stopped by the appearance of a venerable figure seated on the summit of an inaccessible rock, who, with a voice more than human, reproaches the king with all the desolation and misery which he had brought on his country; foretells the misfortunes of the Norman race, and with prophetic spirit declares that all his cruelty shall never extinguish the noble ardour of poetic genius in this island; and that men shall never be wanting to celebrate true virtue and valour in immortal strains, to expose vice and infamous pleasure, and boldly censure tyranny and oppression. His song ended, he precipitates himself from the mountain, and is swallowed up by the river that rolls at its feet."

Mitford, in his "Essay on the Poetry of Gray," says of this Ode: "The tendency of *The Bard* is to show the retributive justice that follows an act of tyranny and wickedness; to denounce on Edward, in his person and his progeny, the effect of the crime he had committed in the massacre of the bards; to convince him that neither his power nor situation could save him from the natural and necessary consequences of his guilt; that not even the virtues which he possessed could atone for the vices with which they were accompanied:

> 'Helm nor hauberk's twisted mail,
> Nor e'en thy *virtues*, tyrant, shall avail.'

This is the real tendency of the poem; and well worthy it was of being adorned and heightened by such a profusion of splendid images and beautiful machinery. We must also observe how much this moral feeling increases as we approach the close; how the poem rises in dignity; and by what a fine gradation the solemnity of the subject ascends. The Bard commenced his song with feelings of sorrow for his departed brethren and his desolate country. This despondence, however, has given way to emotions of a nobler and more exalted nature. What can be more magnificent than the vision which opens before him to display the triumph of justice and the final glory of his cause? And it may be added, what can be more forcible or emphatic than the language in which it is conveyed?

> 'But oh! what solemn scenes on Snowdon's height,
> Descending slow their glittering skirts unroll?
> Visions of glory, spare my aching sight!
> Ye unborn ages, crowd not on my soul!'

The fine apostrophe to the shade of Taliessin completes the picture of exultation:

> 'Hear from the grave, great Taliessin, hear;
> They breathe a soul to animate thy clay.'

The triumph of justice, therefore, is now complete. The vanquished has risen superior to his conqueror, and the reader closes the poem with feelings of content and satisfaction. He has seen the Bard uplifted both by a divine energy and by the natural superiority of virtue; and the conqueror has shrunk into a creature of hatred and abhorrence:

> 'Be thine despair, and sceptred care;
> To triumph, and to die, are mine.'"

With regard to the *obscurity* of the poem, the same writer remarks that "it is such only as of necessity arises from the plan and conduct of a prophecy." "In the prophetic poem," he adds, "one point of history alone is told, and the rest is to be acquired previously by the reader; as in the contemplation of an historical picture, which commands only one moment of time, our memory must supply us with the necessary links of knowledge; and that point of time selected by the painter must be illustrated by the spectator's knowledge of the past or future, of the cause or the consequences."

He refers, for corroboration of this opinion, to Dr. Campbell, who in his "Philosophy of Rhetoric," says: "I know no style to which darkness of a certain sort is more suited than to the prophetical: many reasons might

be assigned which render it improper that prophecy should be perfectly
understood before it be accomplished. Besides, we are certain that a
prediction may be very dark before the accomplishment, and yet so plain
afterwards as scarcely to admit a doubt in regard to the events suggested.
It does not belong to critics to give laws to prophets, nor does it fall within the confines of any human art to lay down rules for a species of composition so far above art. Thus far, however, we may warrantably observe,
that when the prophetic style is imitated in poetry, the piece ought, as much
as possible, to possess the character above mentioned. This character,
in my opinion, is possessed in a very eminent degree by Mr. Gray's ode
called *The Bard*. It is all darkness to one who knows nothing of the
English history posterior to the reign of Edward the First, and all light
to one who is acquainted with that history. But this is a kind of writing
whose peculiarities can scarcely be considered as exceptions from ordinary rules."

Farther on in the same essay, Mitford remarks : " The skill of Gray
is, I think, eminently shown in the superior distinctness with which he
has marked those parts of his prophecies which are speedily to be accomplished ; and in the gradations by which, as he descends, he has
insensibly melted the more remote into the deeper and deeper shadow-
ings of general language. The first prophecy is the fate of Edward the
Second.   In that the Bard has pointed out the very night in which he is
to be destroyed ; has named the river that flowed around his prison, and
the castle that was the scene of his sufferings :

'Mark the *year*, and mark the *night*,
When *Severn* shall re-echo with affright
The shrieks of death thro' Berkeley's roofs that ring,
Shrieks of an agonizing king.'

How different is the imagery when Richard the Second is described ;
and how indistinctly is the luxurious monarch marked out in the form
of the morning, and his country in the figure of the vessel !

'The swarm that in thy noontide beam were born?
Gone to salute the rising morn.
Fair laughs the morn,' etc.

The last prophecy is that of the civil wars, and of the death of the two
young princes. No place, no name is now noted : and all is seen through
the dimness of figurative expression :

'Above, below, the rose of snow,
Twin'd with her blushing foe, we spread :
The bristled boar in infant gore
Wallows beneath the thorny shade.'"

Hales remarks : " It is perhaps scarcely now necessary to say that the
tradition on which *The Bard* is founded is wholly groundless. Edward
I. never did massacre Welsh bards. Their name is legion in the beginning of the 14th century. Miss Williams, the latest historian of Wales,
does not even mention the old story."*

* The *Saturday Review*, for June 19, 1875, in the article from which we have elsewhere quoted (p. 79, foot-note), refers to this point as follows :

1. A good example of alliteration.

2. Cf. Shakes. *K. John*, iv. 2 : " and vast confusion waits."

4. Gray quotes *K. John*, v. 1 : " Mocking the air with colours idly spread."

5. " The hauberk was a texture of steel ringlets, or rings interwoven, forming a coat of mail that sat close to the body, and adapted itself to every motion " (Gray).

Cf. Robert of Gloucester : " With helm and hauberk ;" and Dryden, *Pal. and Arc.* iii. 603 : " Hauberks and helms are hewed with many a wound."

7. *Nightly.* Nocturnal, as often in poetry. Cf. *Il Pens.* 84, etc.

9. *The crested pride.* Gray quotes Dryden, *Indian Queen* : " The crested adder's pride."

11. " Snowdon was a name given by the Saxons to that mountainous tract which the Welsh themselves call *Craigian-eryri :* it included all the highlands of Caernarvonshire and Merionethshire, as far east as the river Conway. R. Hygden, speaking of the castle of Conway, built by King Edward the First, says : 'Ad ortum amnis Conway ad clivum montis Erery ;' and Matthew of Westminster (ad ann. 1283), 'Apud Aberconway ad pedes montis Snowdoniae fecit erigi castrum forte ' " (Gray).

It was in the spring of 1283 that English troops at last forced their way among the defiles of Snowdon. Llewellyn had preserved those passes and heights intact until his death in the preceding December. The surrender of Dolbadern in the April following that dispiriting event opened a way for the invader ; and William de Beauchamp, Earl of Warwick, at once advanced by it (Hales).

The epithet *shaggy* is highly appropriate, as Leland (*Itin.*) says that great woods clothed the mountain in his time. Cf. Dyer, *Ruins of Rome:*

> " as Britannia's oaks
> On Merlin's mount, or Snowdon's rugged sides,
> Stand in the clouds."

See also *Lycidas*, 54 : " Nor on the shaggy top of Mona high ;" and *P. L.* vi. 645 : " the shaggy tops."

" Gray was one of the first writers to show that earlier parts of English history were not only worth attending to, but were capable of poetic treatment. We can almost forgive him for dressing up in his splendid verse a foul and baseless calumny against Edward the First, when we remember that to most of Gray's contemporaries Edward the First must have seemed a person almost mythical, a benighted Popish savage, of whom there was very little to know, and that little hardly worth knowing. Our feeling towards Gray in this matter is much the same as our feeling towards Mitford in the matter of Greek history. We are angry with Mitford for misrepresenting Demosthenes and a crowd of other Athenian worthies, but we do not forget that he was the first to deal with Demosthenes and his fellows, neither as mere names nor as demi-gods, but as real living men like ourselves. It was a pity to misrepresent Demosthenes, but even the misrepresentation was something ; it showed that Demosthenes could be made the subject of human feeling one way or another. It is unpleasant to hear the King whose praise it was that

'Velox est ad veniam, ad vindictam tardus,'

spoken of as 'ruthless,' and the rest of it. But Gray at least felt that Edward was a real man, while to most of his contemporaries he could have been little more than ' the figure of an old Gothic king,' such as Sir Roger de Coverley looked when he sat in Edward's own chair."

13. *Stout Gloster.* "Gilbert de Clare, surnamed the Red, Earl of Gloucester and Hereford, son-in-law to King Edward" (Gray). He had, in 1282, conducted the war in South Wales; and after overthrowing the enemy near Llandeilo Fawr, had reinforced the king in the northwest.

14. *Mortimer.* "Edmond de Mortimer, Lord of Wigmore" (Gray). It was by one of his knights, named Adam de Francton, that Llewellyn, not at first known to be he, was slain near Pont Orewyn (Hales).

On *quivering lance*, cf. Virgil, *Æn.* xii. 94: "hastam quassatque trementem."

15. *On a rock whose haughty brow.* Cf. Daniel, *Civil Wars :* "A huge aspiring rock, whose surly brow."

The *rock* is probably meant for Penmaen-mawr, the northern termination of the Snowdon range. It is a mass of rock, 1545 feet high, a few miles from the mouth of the Conway, the valley of which it overlooks. Towards the sea it presents a rugged and almost perpendicular front. On its summit is Braich-y-Dinas, an ancient fortified post, regarded as the strongest hold of the Britons in the district of Snowdon. Here the reduced bands of the Welsh army were stationed during the negotiation between their prince Llewellyn and Edward I. Within the inner enclosure is a never-failing well of pure water. The rock is now pierced with a tunnel 1890 feet long for the Chester and Holyhead railway.

17. *Rob'd in the sable garb of woe.* It would appear that Wharton had criticised this line, for in a letter to him, dated Aug. 21, 1757, Gray writes: "You may alter that '*Robed in* the sable,' etc., almost in your own words, thus,

> ' With fury pale, and pale with woe,
>   Secure of Fate, the Poet stood,' etc.

Though *haggard*, which conveys to you the idea of a *witch*, is indeed only a metaphor taken from an unreclaimed hawk, which is called a *haggard*, and looks wild and *farouche*, and jealous of its liberty." Gray seems to have afterwards returned to his first (and we think better) reading.

19. "The image was taken from a well-known picture of Raphael, representing the Supreme Being in the vision of Ezekiel. There are two of these paintings (both believed originals), one at Florence, the other in the Duke of Orleans's collection at Paris" (Gray).

20. *Like a meteor.* Gray quotes *P. L.* i. 537: "Shone like a meteor streaming to the wind."

21, 22. Wakefield remarks: "This is poetical language in perfection; and breathes the sublime spirit of Hebrew poetry, which delights in this grand rhetorical substitution."

23. *Desert caves.* Cf. *Lycidas*, 39: "The woods and desert caves."

26. *Hoarser murmurs.* That is, perhaps, with continually increasing hoarseness, hoarser and hoarser; or it may mean with unwonted hoarseness, like the comparative sometimes in Latin (Hales).

28. Hoel is called *high-born*, being the son of Owen Gwynedd, prince of North Wales, by Finnog, an Irish damsel. He was one of his father's generals in his wars against the English, Flemings, and Normans, in South Wales; and was a famous bard, as his poems that are extant testify.

Soft Llewellyn's lay. "The lay celebrating the mild Llewellyn," says

Hales, though he afterwards remarks that, "looking at the context, it would be better to take *Llewellyn* here for a bard." Many bards celebrated the warlike prowess and princely qualities of Llewellyn. A poem by Einion the son of Guigan calls him "a tender-hearted prince;" and another, by Llywarch Brydydd y Moch, says: "Llewellyn, though in battle he killed with fury, though he burned like an outrageous fire, yet was a mild prince when the mead-horns were distributed." In an ode by Llygard Gwr he is also called "Llewellyn the mild."

29. Cadwallo and Urien were bards of whose songs nothing has been preserved. Taliessin (see 121 below) dedicated many poems to the latter, and wrote an elegy on his death: he was slain by treachery in the year 560.

30. *That hush'd the stormy main.* Cf. Shakes. *M. N. D.* ii. 2:

> "Uttering such dulcet and harmonious breath,
> That the rude sea grew civil at her song."

33. *Modred.* This name is not found in the lists of the old bards. It may have been borrowed from the Arthurian legends; or, as Mitford suggests, it may refer to "the famous Myrddin ab Morvyn, called Merlyn the Wild, a disciple of Taliessin, the form of the name being changed for the sake of euphony."

34. *Plinlimmon.* One of the loftiest of the Welsh mountains, being 2463 feet in height. It is really a group of mountains, three of which tower high above the others, and on each of these is a *carnedd*, or pile of stones. The highest of the three is further divided into two peaks, and on these, as well as on another prominent part of the same height, are other piles of stones. These five piles, according to the common tradition, mark the graves of slain warriors, and serve as memorials of their exploits; but some believe that they were intended as landmarks or military signals, and that from them the mountain was called *Pump-lumon* or *Pum-lumon*, "the five beacons"—a name somehow corrupted into *Plinlimmon.* Five rivers take their rise in the recesses of Plinlimmon—the Wye, the Severn, the Rheidol, the Llyfnant, and the Clywedog.

35. *Arvon's shore.* "The shores of Caernarvonshire, opposite the isle of Anglesey" (Gray). *Caernarvon*, or *Caer yn Arvon*, means the camp in Arvon.

38. "Camden and others observe that eagles used annually to build their aerie among the rocks of Snowdon, which from thence (as some think) were named by the Welsh *Craigian-eryri*, or the crags of the eagles. At this day (I am told) the highest point of Snowdon is called *the Eagle's Nest.* That bird is certainly no stranger to this island, as the Scots, and the people of Cumberland, Westmoreland, etc., can testify; it even has built its nest in the peak of Derbyshire [see Willoughby's Ornithology, published by Ray]" (Gray).

40. *Dear as the light.* Cf. Virgil, *Æn.* iv. 31: "O luce magis dilecta sorori."

41. *Dear as the ruddy drops.* Gray quotes Shakes. *J. C.* ii. 1:

> "As dear to me as are the ruddy drops
> That visit my sad heart."

Cf. also Otway, *Venice Preserved:*

> "Dear as the vital warmth that feeds my life,
> Dear as these eyes that weep in fondness o'er thee."

42. Wakefield quotes Pope : "And greatly falling with a fallen state ;" and Dryden : "And couldst not fall but with thy country's fate."

44. *Grisly.* See on *Eton Coll.* 82. Cf. *Lycidas*, 52 :

> "the steep
> Where your old bards, the famous Druids, lie."

48. "See the Norwegian ode that follows" (Gray). This ode (*The Fatal Sisters*, translated from the Norse) describes the *Valkyriur*, "the choosers of the slain," or warlike Fates of the Gothic mythology, as weaving the destinies of those who were doomed to perish in battle. It begins thus :

> "Now the storm begins to lower
> (Haste, the loom of hell prepare),
> Iron sleet of arrowy shower
> Hurtles in the darken'd air.

> "Glittering lances are the loom,
> Where the dusky warp we strain,
> Weaving many a soldier's doom,
> Orkney's woe, and Randver's bane.

> *   *   *   *   *   *   *

> "Shafts for shuttles, dipt in gore,
> Shoot the trembling cords along ;
> Swords, that once a monarch bore,
> Keep the tissue close and strong.

> *   *   *   *   *   *   *

> "(Weave the crimson web of war)
> Let us go, and let us fly,
> Where our friends the conflict share,
> Where they triumph, where they die."

51. Cf. Dryden, *Sebastian*, i. 1 :

> "I have a soul that, like an ample shield,
> Can take in all, and verge enough for more."

55. "Edward the Second, cruelly butchered in Berkeley Castle" (Gray). The 1st ed. and that of 1768 have "roofs ;" the modern eds. "roof."

Berkeley Castle is on the southeast side of the town of Berkeley, on a height commanding a fine view of the Severn and the surrounding country, and is in a state of perfect preservation. It is said to have been founded by Roger de Berkeley soon after the Norman Conquest. About the year 1150 it was granted by Henry II. to Robert Fitzhardinge, Governor of Bristol, who strengthened and enlarged it. On the right of the great staircase leading to the keep, and approached by a gallery, is the room in which it is supposed that Edward II. was murdered, Sept. 21, 1327. The king, during his captivity here, composed a dolorous poem, of which the following is an extract :

> "Moste blessed Jesu,
> Roote of all vertue,
> Graunte I may the sue,
> In all humylyte,

> Sen thou for our good,
> Lyste to shede thy blood,
> An stretche the upon the rood,
> For our iniquyte.
> I the beseche,
> ·Most holsome leche,
> That thou wylt seche
> For me such grace,
> That when my body vyle
> My soule shall exyle
> Thou brynge in short wyle
> It in reste and peace."

Walpole, who visited the place in 1774, says : "The room shown for the murder of Edward II., and the shrieks of an agonizing king, I verily believe to be genuine. It is a dismal chamber, almost at the top of the house, quite detached, and to be approached only by a kind of foot-bridge, and from that descends a large flight of steps, that terminates on strong gates ; exactly a situation for a *corps de garde*."

56. Cf. Hume's description : "The screams with which the agonizing king filled the castle."

57. *She-wolf of France.* "Isabel of France, Edward the Second's adulterous queen" (Gray). Cf. Shakes. 3 *Hen. VI.* i. 4 : "She-wolf of France, but worse than wolves of France ;" and read the context.

60. "Triumphs of Edward the Third in France" (Gray).

61. Cf. Cowley : "Ruin behind him stalks, and empty desolation ;" and Oldham, *Ode to Homer :*

> "Where'er he does his dreadful standard bear,
> Horror stalks in the van, and slaughter in the rear."

63. For *victor* the MS. has "conqueror ;" also in next line " the " for *his ;* and in 65, "what . . . what" for *no . . . no.*

64. "Death of that king, abandoned by his children, and even robbed in his last moments by his courtiers and his mistress" (Gray).

67. "Edward the Black Prince, dead some time before his father" (Gray).

69. The MS. has "hover'd in thy noontide ray," and in the next line "the rising day."

In *Agrippina*, a fragment of a tragedy, published among the posthumous poems of Gray, we have the same figure ;

> "around thee call
> The gilded swarm that wantons in the sunshine
> Of thy full favour."

71. "Magnificence of Richard the Second's reign. See Froissard and other contemporary writers" (Gray).

For this line and the remainder of the stanza, the MS. has the following :

> "Mirrors of Saxon truth and loyalty,
> Your helpless, old, expiring master view !
> They hear not : scarce religion does supply
> Her mutter'd requiems, and her holy dew.
> Yet thou, proud boy, from Pomfret's walls shalt send
> A sigh, and envy oft thy happy grandsire's end."

On the passage as it stands, cf. Shakes. *M. of V.* ii. 6 :

> " How like a younger, or a prodigal,
>   The scarfed bark puts from her native bay," etc.

Also Spenser, *Visions of World's Vanitie,* ix :

> " Looking far foorth into the Ocean wide,
> A goodly ship with banners bravely dight,
> And flag in her top-gallant, I espide
> Through the maine sea making her merry flight.
> Faire blew the winde into her bosome right ;
> And th' heavens looked lovely all the while
> That she did seeme to daunce, as in delight,
> And at her owne felicitie did smile," etc. ;

and again, *Visions of Petrarch,* ii. :

> " After, at sea a tall ship did appeare,
> Made all of heben and white yvorie ;
> The sailes of golde, of silke the tackle were :
> Milde was the winde, calme seem'd the sea to bee,
> The skie eachwhere did show full bright and faire :
> With rich treasures this gay ship fraighted was :
> But sudden storme did so turmoyle the aire,
> And tumbled up the sea, that she (alas)
> Strake on a rock, that under water lay,
> And perished past all recoverie."

See also Milton, *S. A.* 710 foll.

72. *The azure realm.* Cf. Virgil, *Ciris,* 483 : " Caeruleo pollens conjunx Neptunia regno."

73. Note the alliteration. **Cf. Dryden,** *Annus Mirab.* st. **151** :

> "The goodly London, in her gallant trim,
>   The phœnix-daughter of the vanish'd old,
> Like a rich bride does to the ocean swim,
>   And on her shadow rides in floating gold."

75. *Sweeping whirlwind's sway.* Cf. the posthumous fragment by Gray on *Education and Government,* 48 : " And where the deluge burst with sweepy sway." The expression is from Dryden, who uses it repeatedly ; as in *Geo.* i. 483 : " And rolling onwards with a sweepy sway ;" *Ov. Met.:* "Rushing onwards with a sweepy sway ;" *Æn.* vii. : " The branches bend beneath their sweepy sway," etc.

76. *That hush'd in grim repose,* etc. Cf. Dryden, *Sigismonda and Guiscardo,* 242 :

> "So, like a lion that unheeded lay,
> Dissembling sleep, and watchful to betray.
> With inward rage he meditates his prey ;"

and *Absalom and Achitophel,* 447 :

> " And like a lion, slumbering in the way,
> Or sleep dissembling, while he waits his prey."

77. " Richard the Second (as we are told by Archbishop Scroop and the confederate Lords in their manifesto, by Thomas of Walsingham, and all the older writers) was starved to death. The story of his assassination by Sir Piers of Exon is of much later date " (Gray).

79. *Reft of a crown.* Wakefield quotes Mallet's ballad of *William and Margaret*:

> "Such is the robe that kings must wear
> When death has reft their crown."

82. *A baleful smile.* The MS. has "A smile of horror on." Cf. Milton, *P. L.* ii. 846 : "Grinn'd horrible a ghastly smile."

THE TRAITOR'S GATE OF THE TOWER.

83. "Ruinous wars of York and Lancaster" (Gray). Cf. *P. L.* vi. 209 : "Arms on armour clashing brayed."

84. Cf. Shakes. 1 *Hen. IV.* iv. 1 : "Harry to Harry shall, hot horse to horse ;" and Massinger, *Maid of Honour :* "Man to man, and horse to horse."

87. "Henry the Sixth, George Duke of Clarence, Edward the Fifth, Richard Duke of York, etc., believed to be murdered secretly in the Tower of London. The oldest part of that structure is vulgarly attributed to Julius Cæsar" (Gray). The MS. has "Grim towers."

88. *Murther.* See on *murtherous,* p. 105.

89. *His consort.* "Margaret of Anjou, a woman of heroic spirit, who struggled hard to save her husband and her crown" (Gray).

I

HENRY V.

His father. "Henry the Fifth" (Gray).

90. *The meek usurper.* "Henry the Sixth, very near being canonized. The line of Lancaster had no right of inheritance to the crown" (Gray). See on *Eton Coll.* 4. The MS. has "hallow'd head."

91. *The rose of snow,* etc. "The white and red roses, devices of York and Lancaster" (Gray).

Cf. Shakes. 1 *Hen. VI.* ii. 4 :

> "No, Plantagenet,
> 'Tis not for shame, but anger, that thy cheeks
> Blush for pure shame, to counterfeit our roses."

93. *The bristled boar.* "The silver boar was the badge of Richard the Third ; whence he was usually known in his own time by the name of *the Boar*" (Gray). Scott (notes to *Lay of Last Minstrel*) says : "The crest or bearing of a warrior was often used as a *nom de guerre.* Thus Richard III. acquired his well-known epithet, 'the Boar of York.'" Cf. Shakes. *Rich. III.* iv. 5 : "this most bloody boar ;" v. 2 : "The wretched, bloody, and usurping boar," etc.

98. See on 48 above.

99. *Half of thy heart.* "Eleanor of Castile died a few years after the conquest of Wales. The heroic proof she gave of her affection for her

lord is well known.* The monuments of his regret and sorrow for the loss of her † are still to be seen at Northampton, Geddington, Waltham, and other places " (Gray). Cf. Horace, *Od.* i. 3, 8 : " animae dimidium meae."

101. *Nor thus forlorn.* In MS. "nor here forlorn ;" in next line, " Leave your despairing Caradoc to mourn ;" in 103, "yon black clouds ;" in 104, " They sink, they vanish ;" in 105, " But oh ! what scenes of heaven on Snowdon's height ;" in 106, " their golden skirts."

107. Cf. Dryden, *State of Innocence*, iv. 1 : " Their glory shoots upon my aching sight."

109. " It was the common belief of the Welsh nation that King Arthur was still alive in Fairyland, and would return again to reign over Britain " (Gray).

In the MS. this line and the next read thus :

> " From Cambria's thousand hills a thousand strains
> Triumphant tell aloud, another Arthur reigns."

110. " Both Merlin and Taliessin had prophesied that the Welsh should regain their sovereignty over this island; which seemed to be accomplished in the house of Tudor " (Gray).

111. *Many a baron bold.* Cf. *L'Allegro*, 119 : "throngs of knights and barons bold."

The reading in the MS. is,

> " Youthful knights, and barons bold,
> With dazzling helm, and horrent spear."

112. *Their starry fronts.* Cf. Milton, *Ode on the Passion*, 18 : " His starry front ;" Statius, *Theb.* 613 : "Heu ! ubi siderei vultus."

115. *A form divine.* Elizabeth. Wakefield quotes Spenser's eulogy of the queen, *Shep. Kal. Apr.:*

> "Tell me, have ye seene her angelick face,
> Like Phœbe fayre?
> Her heavenly haveour, her princely grace,
> Can you well compare?
> The Redde rose medled with the White yfere,
> In either cheeke depeincten lively chere ;
> Her modest eye,
> Her Majestie,
> Where have you seene the like but there ?"

---

* See Tennyson, *Dream of Fair Women:*

> "Or her who knew that Love can vanquish Death,
> Who kneeling, with one arm about her king,
> Drew forth the poison with her balmy breath,
> Sweet as new buds in spring."

† Gray refers to the " Eleanor crosses," erected at the places where the funeral procession halted each night on the journey from Hardby, in Nottinghamshire (near Lincoln), where the queen died, to Westminster. Of the thirteen (or, as some say, fifteen) crosses only three now remain—at Northampton, Geddington, and Waltham. The one at Charing Cross in London has been replaced by a fac-simile of the original. These monuments were all exquisite works of Gothic art, fitting memorials of *la chère Reine,* " the beloved of all England," as Walsingham calls her.

117. " Speed, relating an audience given by Queen Elizabeth to Paul Dzialinski, ambassador of Poland, says : ' And thus she, lion-like rising, daunted the malapert orator no less with her stately port and majestical deporture, than with the tartnesse of her princelie checkes ' " (Gray). The MS. reads " A lion-port, an awe-commanding face."

121. " Taliessin, chief of the bards, flourished in the sixth century. His works are still preserved, and his memory held in high veneration among his countrymen " (Gray).

As Hales remarks, there is no authority for connecting him with Arthur, as Tennyson does in his *Holy Grail.*

123. Cf. Congreve, *Ode to Lord Godolphin :* " And soars with rapture while she sings."

124. *The eye of heaven.* Wakefield quotes Spenser, *F. Q.* 1. 3. 4,

> " Her angel's face
> As the great eye of heaven shined bright."

Cf. Shakes. *Rich. II.* iii. 2 : " the searching eye of heaven."

Many-colour'd wings. Cf. Shakes. *Temp.* iv. 1 : " Hail, many-colour'd messenger ;" and Milton, *P. L.* iii. 642 :

> " Wings he wore
> Of many a colour'd plume sprinkled with gold.''

126. Gray quotes Spenser, *F. Q.* Proeme, 9 :

> " Fierce warres and faithful loves shall moralize my song.''

128. " Shakespeare " (Gray). Cf. *Il Penseroso,* 102 : " the buskin'd stage ;" that is, the tragic stage.

129. *Pleasing pain.* Cf. Spenser, *F. Q.* vi. 9, 10 : " sweet pleasing payne ;" and Dryden, *Virg. Ecl.* iii. 171 : " Pleasing pains of love."

131. " Milton " (Gray).

133. " The succession of poets after Milton's time " (Gray).

135. *Fond.* Foolish. See on *Prog. of Poesy,* 46.

On the couplet, cf. Dekker, *If this be not a good play,* etc. :

> " Thinkest thou, base lord,
> Because the glorious sun behind black clouds
> Has awhile hid his beams, he's darken'd forever,
> Eclips'd never more to shine ?''

137. Cf. *Lycidas,* 169 : " And yet anon repairs his drooping head ;" and Fletcher, *Purple Island,* vi. 64 : " So soon repairs her light, trebling her new-born raies."

141. Mitford remarks that there is a passage (which he misquotes, as usual) in the *Thebaid* of Statius (iii. 81) similar to this, describing a bard who had survived his companions :

> " Sed jam nudaverat ensem
> Magnanimus vates, et nunc trucis ora tyranni,
> Nunc ferrum adspectans : ' Nunquam tibi sanguinis hujus
> Jus erit, aut magno feries imperdita Tydeo
> Pectora ; *vado equidem exsultans et ereptaque fata*
> Insequor, et comites feror expectatus ad umbras ;
> *Te* Superis, fratrique.' Et jam media orsa loquentis
> Abstulerat plenum capulo latus."

Cf. also a passage in Pindar (*Olymp.* i. 184), which Gray seems to have had in mind :

> Εἴη σὲ τε τοῦτον
> Ὑψοῦ χρόνον πατεῖν, ἐμέ
> Τε τοσσάδε νικαφόροις
> Ὁμιλεῖν, κ. τ. λ.

143. Cf. Virgil, *Ecl.* viii. 59 :

> "Praeceps aërii specula de montis in undas
> Deferar; extremum hoc munus morientis habeto."

As we have given Johnson's criticism on *The Progress of Poesy*, we append his comments on this " Sister Ode :"

" 'The Bard' appears, at the first view, to be, as Algarotti and others have remarked, an imitation of the prophecy of Nereus. Algarotti thinks it superior to its original ; and, if preference depends only on the imagery and animation of the two poems, his judgment is right. There is in 'The Bard' more force, more thought, and more variety. But to copy is less than to invent, and the copy has been unhappily produced at a wrong time. The fiction of Horace was to the Romans credible ; but its revival disgusts us with apparent and unconquerable falsehood. *Incredulus odi.*

" To select a singular event, and swell it to a giant's bulk by fabulous appendages of spectres and predictions, has little difficulty ; for he that forsakes the probable may always find the marvellous. And it has little use ; we are affected only as we believe ; we are improved only as we find something to be imitated or declined. I do not see that ' The Bard' promotes any truth, moral or political.

" His stanzas are too long, especially his epodes ; the ode is finished before the ear has learned its measures, and consequently before it can receive pleasure from their consonance and recurrence.

" Of the first stanza the abrupt beginning has been celebrated ; but technical beauties can give praise only to the inventor. It is in the power of any man to rush abruptly upon his subject, that has read the ballad of 'Johnny Armstrong,'

> 'Is there ever a man in all Scotland—'

" The initial resemblances, or alliterations, ' ruin, ruthless, helm or hauberk,' are below the grandeur of a poem that endeavours at sublimity.

" In the second stanza the Bard is well described ; but in the third we have the puerilities of obsolete mythology. When we are told that ' Cadwallo hush'd the stormy main,' and that ' Modred made huge Plinlimmon bow his cloud-topt head,' attention recoils from the repetition of a tale that, even when it was first heard, was heard with scorn.

" The *weaving* of the *winding-sheet* he borrowed, as he owns, from the Northern Bards ; but their texture, however, was very properly the work of female powers, as the act of spinning the thread of life is another mythology. Theft is always dangerous ; Gray has made weavers of slaughtered bards by a fiction outrageous and incongruous. They are then called upon to ' Weave the warp, and weave the woof,' perhaps with no great propriety; for it is by crossing the *woof* with the *warp* that men weave the *web* or piece; and the first line was dearly bought by the admission of its wretched correspondent, 'Give ample room and verge enough.' He has, however, no other line as bad.

"The third stanza of the second ternary is commended, I think, beyond its merit. The personification is indistinct. *Thirst* and *Hunger* are not alike; and their features, to make the imagery perfect, should have been discriminated. We are told, in the same stanza, how 'towers are fed.' But I will no longer look for particular faults; yet let it be observed that the ode might have been concluded with an action of better example; but suicide is always to be had, without expense of thought."

" Ye towers of Julius, London's lasting shame."

HEAD OF OLYMPIAN JOVE.

HYMN TO ADVERSITY.

THIS poem first appeared in Dodsley's *Collection*, vol. iv., together with the "Elegy in a Country Churchyard." In Mason's and Wakefield's editions it is called an "Ode," but the title given by the author is as above.

The motto from Æschylus is not in Dodsley, but appears in the first edition of the poems (1768) in the form given in the text. The best modern editions· of Æschylus have the reading, τὸν (some, τῷ) πάθει μάθος. Keck translates the passage into German thus :

> "Ihn der uns zur Sinnigkeit
> leitet, ihn der fest den Satz
> Stellet, 'Lehre durch das Leid.'"

Plumptre puts it into English as follows :

> "Yea, Zeus, who leadeth men in wisdom's way,
> And fixeth fast the law
> Wisdom by pain to gain.'"

Cf. Mrs. Browning's *Vision of Poets:*

> "Knowledge by suffering entereth.
> And life is perfected by death."

1. Mitford remarks : "Ἄτη, who may be called the goddess of Adversity, is said by Homer to be the daughter of Jupiter (*Il.* τ. 91 : πρέσβα Διὸς θυγάτηρ Ἄτη, ἥ πάντας ἀᾶται). Perhaps, however, Gray only alluded to the passage of Æschylus which he quoted, and which describes Affliction as sent by Jupiter for the benefit of man." The latter is the more probable explanation.

2. Mitford quotes Pope, *Dunciad*, i. 163 : " Then he : ' Great tamer of all human art.' "

3. *Torturing hour.* Cf. Milton, *P. L.* ii. 90 :

> "The vassals of his anger, when the scourge
> Inexorable, and the torturing hour,
> Calls us to penance."

5. *Adamantine chains.* Wakefield quotes Æschylus, *Prom. Vinct.* vi. : Ἀδαμαντίνων δεσμῶν ἐν ἀρρήκτοις πέδαις. Cf. Milton, *P. L.* i. 48 : " In adamantine chains and penal fire ;" and Pope, *Messiah*, 47 : " In adamantine chains shall Death be bound."

6. *Purple tyrants.* Cf. Pope, *Two Choruses to Tragedy of Brutus* : " Till some new tyrant lifts his purple hand." Wakefield cites Horace, *Od.* i. 35, 12 : " Purpurei metuunt tyranni."

8. *With pangs unfelt before.* Cf. Milton, *P. L.* ii. 703 : " Strange horror seize thee, and pangs unfelt before."

9–12. Cf. Bacon, *Essays*, v. (ed. 1625) : " Certainly, Vertue is like pretious Odours, most fragrant when they are incensed [that is, burned], or crushed :* For *Prosperity* doth best discover Vice ;† But *Adversity* doth best discover Vertue."

Cf. also Thomson :

> " If Misfortune comes, she brings along
> The bravest virtues. And so many great
> Illustrious spirits have convers'd with woe,
> Have in her school been taught, as are enough
> To consecrate distress, and make ambition
> E'en wish the frown beyond the smile of fortune."

16. Cf. Virgil, *Æn.* i. 630 : " Non ignara mali, miseris succurrere disco."

18. *Folly's idle brood.* Cf. the opening lines of *Il Penseroso* :

> " Hence, vain deluding Joys,
> The brood of Folly, without father bred !"

20. Mitford quotes Oldham, *Ode :* " And know I have not yet the leisure to be good."

21. *The summer friend.* Cf. Geo. Herbert, *Temple :* " like summer friends, flies of estates and sunshine ;" Quarles, *Sion's Elegies*, xix. : " Ah, summer friendship with the summer ends ;" Massinger, *Maid of Honour :* " O summer friendship." See also Shakespeare, *T. of A.* iii. 6 :

" *2d Lord.* The swallow follows not summer more willing than we your lordship.

" *Timon* [*aside*]. Nor more willingly leaves winter ; such summer-birds are men ;"
and *T. and C.* iii. 3 :

---

* So in his *Apophthegms*, 253, Bacon says : " Mr. Bettenham said ; that virtuous men were like some herbs and spices, that give not their sweet smell till they be broken or crushed."

† Cf. Shakespeare, *Julius Cæsar*, ii. 1 : " It is the bright day that brings forth the adder."

> "For men, like butterflies,
> Shew not their mealy wings but to the summer."

Mitford suggests that Gray had in mind Horace, *Od.* i. 35, 25 :

> "At vulgus infidum et meretrix retro
> Perjura cedit ; diffugiunt cadis
> Cum faece siccatis amici
> Ferre jugum pariter dolosi."

25. *In sable garb.* Cf. Milton, *Il Pens.* 16 : " O'erlaid with black, staid Wisdom's hue."

28. *With leaden eye.* Evidently suggested by Milton's description of Melancholy, *Il Pens.* 43 :

> "Thy rapt soul sitting in thine eyes ;
> There, held in holy passion still,
> Forget thyself to marble, till
> With a sad leaden downward cast
> Thou fix them on the earth as fast."

Mitford cites Sidney, *Astrophel and Stella*, song 7 : " So leaden eyes ;" Dryden, *Cymon and Iphigenia*, 57 : " And stupid eyes that ever lov'd the ground ;" Shakespeare, *Pericles*, i. 2 : " The sad companion, dull-eyed Melancholy ;" and *L. L. L.* iv. 3 : " In leaden contemplation." Cf. also *The Bard*, 69, 70.

31. *To herself severe.* Cf. Carew :

> "To servants kind, to friendship dear,
> To nothing but herself severe ;"

and Dryden : " Forgiving others, to himself severe ;" and Waller : " The Muses' friend, unto himself severe." Mitford quotes several other similar passages.

32. *The sadly pleasing tear.* Rogers cites Dryden's " sadly pleasing thought " (Virgil's *Æn.* x.) ; and Mitford compares Thomson's " lenient, not unpleasing tear."

35. *Gorgon terrors.* Cf. Milton, *P. L.* ii. 611 : " Medusa with Gorgonian terror."

36–40. Cf. *Ode on Eton College*, 55–70 and 81–90.

46–49. Cf. Shakespeare, *As You Like It*, ii. 1 :

> "these are counsellors
> That feelingly persuade me what I am.
> Sweet are the uses of adversity,
> Which, like the toad, ugly and venomous,
> Wears yet a precious jewel in his head ;"

and Mallet :

> "Who hath not known ill-fortune, never knew
> Himself, or his own virtue."

Guizot, in his *Cromwell*, says : " The effect of supreme and irrevocable misfortune is to elevate those souls which it does not deprive of all virtue ;" and Sir Philip Sidney remarks : " A noble heart, like the sun, showeth its greatest countenance in its lowest estate."

" Now rolling down the steep amain,
 Headlong, impetuous, see it pour;
 The rocks and nodding groves rebellow to the roar."
 The Progress of Poesy, 10.

APPENDIX TO NOTES.

JUST as this book is going to press we have received *The Quarterly Review* (London) for January, 1876, which contains an interesting paper on "Wordsworth and Gray." After quoting Wordsworth's remark that "Gray was at the head of those poets who, by their reasonings, have attempted to widen the space of separation between prose and metrical composition, and was, more than any other man, curiously elaborate in the construction of his own poetic diction," the reviewer remarks:

"The indictment, then, brought by Wordsworth against Gray is two-fold. Gray, it seems, had in the first place a false conception of the nature of poetry; and, secondly, a false standard of poetical diction. To begin with the first count, Gray, we are told, sought to widen the space of separation betwixt prose and metrical composition. What this charge amounts to we shall see hereafter. Meantime, did Wordsworth think that between prose and poetry there was any line of demarcation at all? In the Preface [to the "Lyrical Ballads"] from which we have quoted we read:

"'There neither is nor can be any essential difference between the language of prose and metrical composition. We are fond of tracing the resemblance between Poetry and Painting, and accordingly we call them sisters; but where shall we find bonds of connection sufficiently strong to typify the connection betwixt prose and metrical composition?'

"Now this question admits of a very definite answer. Take the Iliad of Homer and a proposition of Euclid. Is it conceivable that the latter could have been expressed at all in metre, or the former expressed half so well in prose? If not, what is the reason? Is it not plain that the poem contains a predominant element of imagination and feeling which is absolutely excluded from the proposition? And in the same way it may be shown that whenever a man expresses himself properly in metre, the subject-matter of his composition belongs to imagination or feeling; whenever he writes in prose his subject belongs to or (if the prose be fiction) intimately resembles matter of fact. We may decide then with certainty that the sphere of poetry lies in Imagination, and that the larger the amount of *just* liberty the Imagination enjoys, the better will be the poetry it produces. But then a further question arises, and this is the key of the whole position, How far does this liberty extend? Is Imagination absolute, supreme, and uncontrolled in its own sphere, or is it under the guidance and government of reason? That its dominion is not universal is obvious, but of its influence we are all conscious, and there is no exaggeration in the eloquent words of Pascal:

" ' This mighty power, the perpetual antagonist of reason, which delights to show its ascendency by bringing her under its control and dominion, has created a second nature in man. It has its joys and its sorrows ; its health, its sickness ; its wealth, its poverty ; it compels reason, in spite of herself, to believe, to doubt, to deny ; it suspends the exercise of the senses, and imparts to them again an artificial acuteness ; it has its follies and its wisdom ; and the most perverse thing of all is that it fills its votaries with a complacency more full and complete even than that which reason can supply.'

" If such be the force of Imagination in active life, how absolute must be its dominion in poetry ! And absolute it is, if we are to believe Wordsworth, who defines poetry to be ' the spontaneous overflow of powerful emotion.' This definition coincides well with modern notions on the nature of the art. But how different is the view if we turn from theory to practice ! It would surely be a serious mistake to describe the noblest poems, like the 'Æneid ' or ' Paradise Lost,' as the product of mere spontaneous emotion. And even in lyric verse, to which it may be said Wordsworth is specially alluding, we find the greatest poets, like Pindar and Simonides, composing their odes for set occasions like the public games, in honour of persons with whom they were but little acquainted, and (most significant fact of all) in the expectation of receiving liberal rewards. We need not say that such considerations detract nothing from the genius of these great poets ; but they prove very conclusively that poetry is not what Wordsworth's definition asserts, and what in these days it is too often assumed to be, the mere gush of unconscious inspiration. The definition of Wordsworth may perhaps suit short lyrics, such as he was himself in the habit of composing, but it would be fatal to the claims of poetry to rank among the higher arts, for it would exclude that quality which, in poetry as in all art, is truly sovereign, Invention. The poet, no less than the mechanical inventor, excels by the exercise of reason, by his knowledge of the required effect, his power of adapting means to ends, and his skill in availing himself of circumstances. Consider for a moment the external difficulties which restrict the poet's liberty, and require the most vigorous efforts of reason to subdue them. To begin with, in order to secure the happy result promised by Horace,

> ' Cui lecta potenter erit res
> Nec facundia deseret hunc nec lucidus ordŏ,'

he has to take the exact measure of his own powers. How many a poet has failed for want of judgment by trespassing on a subject and style for which his genius is unfitted ! Again, he is confronted by the most obvious difficulties of language and metre, which limit his freedom to a degree unknown to the prose-writer. And beyond this, if he wishes to be read— and a poem without readers is no more than a musical instrument without a musician—he has to consider the character of his audience. He must have all the instinct of an orator, all the intuitive knowledge of the world, as well as all the practical resource, which are required to gain command over the hearts of men, and to subdue, by the charms of eloquence, their passions, their prejudices, and their judgment. To achieve such results something more is required than 'the spontaneous overflow of powerful feeling.'

" How far Wordsworth's own poetry illustrates his principles we shall consider presently ; meantime his definition helps us to understand what he meant by Gray's fault of widening the space of separation betwixt prose and metrical composition. Neither in respect of the quantity nor the quality of his verse could Gray's manner of composition be described as spontaneous. Compared with Wordsworth's numerous volumes of poetry, the slender volume that contains the poetry of Gray looks meagre indeed ; yet almost every poem in this small collection is a considered work of art. To begin with 'The Bard.' Few readers, we suppose, would rise from this ode without a sense of its poetical 'effect.' The details may be thought to require too much attention ; the allusions, from the nature of the subject, are, no doubt, difficult ; but a feeling of loftiness, of harmony, of proportion, remains in the mind at the close of the poem, which is not likely to pass away. How, then, was this effect produced ? First of all we see that Gray had selected a good subject ; his raw materials, so to speak, were poetical. The imagination, unembarrassed by common associations, breathes freely in its own region, and is instinctively elevated as it moves among the great events of the past, dwelling on the misfortunes of monarchs, the rise of dynasties, and the splendours of literature. But, in the second place, when he has chosen his subject, it is the part of the poet to impress the great ideas derived from it on the feelings and the memory by the distinctness of the form under which he presents it ; and here poetical invention first begins to work. By the imaginative fiction of 'The Bard,' Gray is enabled to cast the whole course of English history into the form of a prophecy, and to excite the patriotic feelings of the reader, as Virgil roused the pride of his own countrymen by Anchises' forecast of the grandeur of Rome. Finally, when the main design of the poem is thus conceived, observe with what art all the different parts are made to emphasize the beauty of the general conception ; with what dramatic propriety the calamities of the conquering Plantagenet are prophesied by his vanquished foe ; while on the other hand, the literary glories of the Tudor Elizabeth awaken the triumph of the patriot and the poet ; how martial and spirited is the opening of the poem ! how lofty and enthusiastic its close ! Perhaps there is no English lyric which, animated by equal fervour, displays so much architectural genius as 'The Bard.'

" Take, again, the 'Ode on the Prospect of Eton College.' A subject better adapted for the indulgence of personal feeling, or for those sentimental confidences between the reader and the poet, in which the modern muse so much delights, could not be imagined. But what do we find ? The theme is treated in the most general manner. Though emphasizing the irony of his reflection by the beautiful touch of memory in the second stanza, the poet speaks throughout as a moralist or spectator ; from first to last he seems to lose all thought of himself in contemplating the tragedies he foresees for others ; the subject is in fact handled with the most skilful rhetoric, and every stanza is made to strengthen and elaborate the leading thought. In the 'Progress of Poesy,' though the general constructive effect is perhaps inferior to 'The Bard,' we see the same evidence of careful preconsideration, while the course of the poem is particularly distinguished by the beauty of the transitions. Of the form of the ‘ Elegy’ it is superfluous to speak ; a poem so dignified and yet so tender, appeals immediately, and will continue to appeal, to the heart of every English-man, so long as the care of public liberty and love of the soil maintain their hold in this country. In this poem, as indeed in all that Gray ever wrote, we find it his first principle *to prefer his subject to himself ;* he never forgot that while he was a man he was also an artist, and he knew that the function of art was not merely to indulge nature, but to dignify and refine it.

“ Yet, in spite of his love of form, there is nothing frigid or statuesque in the genius of Gray. A vein of deep melancholy, evidently constitu-tional, runs through his poetry, and, considering how little he produced, the number of personal allusions in his verses is undoubtedly large. But he is entirely free from that egotism which we have had frequent occasion to blame as the prevailing vice of modern poetry. For whereas the mod-ern poet thrusts his private feelings into prominence, and finds a luxury in the confession of his sorrows, Gray’s references to himself are intro-duced on public grounds, or, in other words, with a view to poetical effect. He, like our own bards, is ‘ condemned to groan,’ but for different reasons—

> ‘The tender for *another’s* pain,
> The unfeeling for his own.’

“ We have already remarked on the public character of the ‘ Ode on Eton College ;’ but the second stanza of this poem is a pure expression of individual feeling :

> ‘ Ah, happy hills ! ah, pleasing shade !
>   Ah, fields belov’d in vain !
> Where once my careless childhood play’d,
>   A stranger yet to pain !
> I feel the gales that from ye blow
> A momentary bliss bestow,
>   As waving fresh their gladsome wing,
> My weary soul they seem to soothe,
> And, redolent of joy and youth,
>   To breathe a second spring.’

Every one will perceive the art which enforces the truth of the general reflections that follow by the personal experience of the speaker. Again, the ‘ Progress of Poesy’ closes with a personal allusion which, as it is a climax, might, if ill-managed, have appeared arrogant, but which is, in fact, a masterpiece of oratory. After confessing his own inferiority to Pindar, the poet proceeds :

> ‘ Yet oft before his infant eyes would run
>   Such forms as glitter in the Muse’s ray,
> With orient hues, unborrow’d of the sun ;
>   Yet shall he mount, and keep his distant way,
> Beyond the limits of a vulgar fate,
> Beneath the Good how far—but far above the Great !’

There is something very noble in the elevated manner in which the self-complacent triumph of genius, expressed by so many poets from Ennius downwards, is at once justified and chastened by the reflection in these lines. We see in them that the poet alludes to himself in the third person, and he repeats this style in the 'Elegy,' where, after the fourth line, the first personal pronoun is never again used. How just and beautiful is the turn where, after contemplating the general lot of the lowly society he is celebrating, he proceeds to identify his own fate with theirs:

> 'For *thee*, who, mindful of th' unhonour'd dead,
>   Dost in these lines their artless tale relate,
> If, chance, by lonely contemplation led,
>   Some kindred spirit shall inquire thy fate,

> 'Haply some hoary-headed swain may say,' etc.

"The two great characteristics of Gray's poetry that we have noticed—his self-suppression and his sense of form and dignity—are best described by the word 'classical.' What we particularly admire in the great authors of Greece and Rome is their public spirit. Their writings are full of patriotism, good-breeding, and common-sense, and have that happy mixture of art and nature which is only acquired by men who have learned from liberty how to discipline individual instincts by social refinement. Their style is masculine, clear, and moderate; they seem, as it were, never to lose the sense of being before an audience, and, like orators who know that they are always exposed to the judgment of their intellectual equals, they aim at putting intelligible thoughts into the most natural and forcible words. Precisely the same qualities are observable in all the best English writers of the eighteenth century. Addison, Pope, and Goldsmith are perhaps the most shining examples, but the rest are 'classical' in the sense which we have just indicated; and we can hardly be wrong in ascribing this common rhetorical instinct to the intimate connection between the men of thought and the men of action, which existed both in the free states of antiquity, and in England under the rule of the aristocracy. With the advance of the eighteenth century the instinct in English literature seems to grow weaker; the style of our authors becomes more formal and constrained, and symptoms of that dislike of society encouraged by the philosophy of Rousseau more frequently betray themselves. As the poetry of Cowper shows less social instinct than that of Gray, so Gray himself is inferior in this respect to Pope and Goldsmith. But his style has the same lofty public spirit that distinguishes his favourite models, and no worthier form could be imagined to express the ardour excited in the heart of a patriotic poet by the rising fortunes of his native country. We feel that it is in every way fitting that the author of the 'Elegy' should have been the favourite of Wolfe and the countryman of Chatham."

CLIO, THE MUSE OF HISTORY.

INDEX OF WORDS EXPLAINED.

K

www.ingramcontent.com/pod-product-compliance
Lightning Source LLC
Chambersburg PA
CBHW020236030726
47497CB00009B/3115